PARANORMAL COZY MYSTERY

Ropes & Last Hopes

TRIXIE SILVERTALE

Sittin' On A Goldmine
Productions L.L.C.

Sittin' On A Goldmine Productions, L.L.C.

pr@sittinonagoldmine.co

www.sittinonagoldmine.co

ISBN: 978-1-952739-75-0

Cover Design © Sittin' On A Goldmine Productions, L.L.C.

Cover design by Melony Paradise of Paradise Cover Design

Trixie Silvertale
Ropes and Last Hopes: Paranormal Cozy Mystery : a novella / by
Trixie Silvertale — 1st ed.
[1. Paranormal Cozy Mystery — Fiction. 2. Cozy Mystery —

Fiction. 3. Amateur Sleuths — Fiction. 4. Female Sleuth — Fiction. 5. Wit and Humor — Fiction.] 1. Title.

CHAPTER 1

Never marry your best friend, they say. Well, I have good news for the pundits: I'm not. My best friend is a ghost.

The aforementioned ghost happens to be tethered to my bookshop and is the spirit of my amazing grandmother, Myrtle Isadora, who died several years ago and, in her last will and testament, left everything to a granddaughter she'd never met.

When I stepped off a smelly bus that hauled me from Arizona to almost-Canada, I figured it would be a good old-fashioned "turn and burn."

My plan was to assess what she had left me, take whatever I could pawn or sell outright, and head straight back to the cactus-laden Southwest.

Fate made plenty of other arrangements.

I wandered into the town's one-and-only diner

to answer the call of the fry and literally tripped and fell on Sheriff Too-Hot-To-Handle.

Fate: 1. Mitzy Moon: 0.

Next thing you know, I'm unlocking my three-story bookshop, complete with printing museum and secret swanky apartment! The place is fantastic and definitely one of the big reasons why I stuck around.

However, I didn't truly make up my mind to stay until a feisty wildcat scared the bejeezus out of me, and the ghost of my grandmother appeared before my shocked grey eyes.

Fate: 3. Mitzy Moon: 0.

Oh sure, I toyed with the idea of making a run for the border, but once I'd made that connection with family, I couldn't turn back.

You see, I lost my mother at the tender age of eleven. After growing up an orphan and bouncing around mostly not-great foster homes, the miraculous existence of a brand new family changed my whole outlook on life.

CUT TO —
My former life as a film-school dropout and broke barista faded into distant memory as I settled into the Bell, Book & Candle bookshop and the rest of my inheritance. Not only am I a wealthy heiress

that runs a charitable foundation focused on doing good things for my community, but also an antique mood ring my grandmother left me triggered latent psychic abilities.

The ring is vintage 70s with a smoky-black cabochon in the center of gold braided trim, and it randomly shows me snippets of imagery meant to encourage my extrasensory perceptions. It took me a good long time to figure out exactly how those abilities worked and when they could be best employed, but eventually, I got the hang of it — with a little guidance.

My lawyer, Silas Willoughby, also serves as my mentor in all things alchemical and paranormal. His wisdom and patience keep me grounded. Plus, he adores my bookshop's massive collection of tomes filled with arcane knowledge. In fact, he spends a great deal of time in the Rare Books Loft on the mezzanine of my bookstore.

But if you're new to Pin Cherry Harbor, you must be waiting for your own reason to stay.

Here it is: I'm a corpse magnet.

Not literally! I mean, I don't walk down the street having dead bodies rise from the grave and stick to me like silly refrigerator décor. But trouble does seem to follow on my heels.

I'm not particularly comfortable with crime scenes, or any type of disgusting evidence. So I've learned to turn my psychic abilities up or down depending on the situation.

Spoiler alert: After a series of relationship mishaps, the sexy local sheriff and I eventually found a successful dating rhythm. I happily call him my boyfriend. Wait, make that: fiancé!

Trust me, it took some doing! But with the expertise of my grandmother, who possesses multiple ex-spouses, I finally landed the big fish.

I don't mean to make light of the situation, but Sheriff Erick Harper is a catch. He's intelligent, kindhearted, takes care of his mother, protects an entire county — it doesn't hurt that he knows exactly how to fill out a pair of jeans — and has the bluest eyes I've ever seen!

"Grams? Grams? I know you're here. You may be hiding just out of the visual spectrum, but I sense your energy lurking."

Ghost-ma pops into sight with a crackle, like static electricity. "Oh, Mitzy! I should know better than to try and fool you. You were saying such nice things about me. I couldn't resist."

"Saying? I wasn't saying anything, Isadora. I was silently reflecting on how fortunate I am to have stumbled into the life I enjoy in Pin Cherry Harbor. However, since my lips weren't moving, and we have very strict rules about ghostly thought-dropping, you shouldn't have heard anything."

"Reow." Can confirm.

"See? Even Pyewacket agrees with me."

My tan half-wild caracal nods in an entirely too human way, twitches his black-tufted ears, and leaps onto my antique four-poster bed. This mysterious feline is always poking his whiskers into my business and dropping inexplicable — yet surprisingly helpful — clues directly in my sleuthing path.

Grams waves her bejeweled hands dismissively. "Don't you two gang up on me. All bets are off now that you're engaged, sweetie. I have to stay close to make sure I don't miss any important potential wedding details!"

"Seriously? You've tried that excuse before, Grams. I'm not the one planning the wedding. I gave you a very short list of musts, and permission to go hog-wild with the rest. So there's absolutely no way you could miss something that you're responsible for planning. No. Thought. Dropping."

The elegant ghost crosses her arms over her burgundy silk-and-tulle Marchesa burial gown. She casually adjusts one of her many strands of pearls and frowns. "I'll do my best, dear. You know how muddled up I get."

Walking through her to push the twisted ivy medallion on the wall inside the apartment next to the secret bookcase door, I toss a reply over my shoulder. "I know how muddled up you *pretend* to get."

When the door reaches the end of its slide, I step onto the thick Persian carpets in the Rare Books Loft. Dragging my fingers along meticulously aligned oak reading tables, I walk toward a brass lamp that has carelessly been left on. Reaching under the green-glass shade, I pull the chain, turn the light off, and proceed to the wrought-iron circular staircase. When I reach the bottom, I unhook the chain with its bold "No Admittance" sign and quickly hook it behind me before triggering the alarm.

"I was hoping you'd try to jump. I could use a good laugh."

That would be my volunteer employee, Twiggy. She was my grandmother's best friend in life and works at the bookshop for the simple payment of front-row seats to my mishaps. Which, to be fair, are many. Now that Erick and I have locked down our relationship, my love life catastrophes are more limited, but my natural clumsiness still offers her plenty to cackle about.

Pyewacket rockets past me and sits impatiently in front of the cabinet that holds his favorite treat, a sugary children's cereal called Fruity Puffs.

Pye comes and goes as he pleases, and I have no interest in knowing what happens when he's out of my sight. I'm sure there are several birds, rodents, and bunnies who regret not seeing him coming.

In my presence, he simply eats this adorable snack. It goes a long way toward helping me believe in his innate cuddliness. Probably why Grams ended up giving him the nickname Mr. Cuddlekins.

CHAPTER 2

Living the life of a wealthy heiress in a quaint northern town in almost-Canada isn't all hats and horns. There's always the part where the ghost of my grandmother dresses me like a living doll in her favorite high-fashion pieces, which results in frequent trips to the local dry cleaner.

Trust me, when I was scraping my pennies together to pay rent back in Arizona, my clothes were lucky to get a hand wash in the bathroom sink! Now, frequent walks to the local dry-cleaning establishment with an armload of couture, are commonplace.

The frozen great lake nestled in the harbor behind my bookshop is playing nice today. The temperature is magically above zero, and the wind is keeping its worst at bay. The short stroll to the cleaners is — dare I say — pleasant.

As I approach Harbor Cleaners, the presence of police tape over the door sends a shock wave of psychic messages flooding through my senses.

Someone's dead!

It's Tanya!

Oh, my gosh! She suffocated —

Using one of the exercises Silas Willoughby taught me, I close off my special abilities. These are not images I want floating through my brain. Without thinking, I cross the crime scene tape and enter the dry-cleaning establishment.

As though I haven't lived in town for over three years, Deputy Paulsen turns on her stout legs and pulls her gun. "Not today. Crime scene. Official personnel only."

Why does this bully with a badge always wanna fight me? "Good morning, Deputy Paulsen. I think honorary deputy is an official title. It may have been handed to me as somewhat of a joke, but I take it seriously. What are we looking at here? A 187? A 5150? Possible 234?"

She grumbles and holsters her weapon, but her right-hand remains firmly on the grip. "Sheriff Harper is in the back. Don't touch anything, Moon."

"I wouldn't dream of it, Deputy."

Now that I've received an unofficial invitation into the crime scene, I toss my snow-white hair and carefully pick my way through the piles of bagged clothing that were yanked from the rotating dry-cleaning rack.

Clear signs of a struggle.

Whoever attacked Tanya had their work cut out for them. There are fingernail scratches marking the opposite wall and a fair number of articles of clothing on the floor. She must've grabbed anything she could get her hands on in an attempt to fight off her attacker.

At the sound of crinkling plastic, Sheriff Harper looks up from the body. "Moon, what are you doing in here? This is a crime scene."

"Yeah, I gathered that. Maybe I can help."

The muscles in his handsome jaw clench and release as he gets to his feet. He leaves the medical examiner to continue her work and steps uncomfortably close to me.

The woodsy-citrus scent of his nearness always does me in. If there weren't a corpse five feet away, I might be tempted to indulge in a public display of affection. However, my tummy is currently tumbling in a far more nausea-adjacent fashion.

"Mitzy, we've talked about this more than once. It's not appropriate for you to be insinuating yourself into crime scenes."

"I would hardly call it insinuating, Sheriff Harper. I simply reminded Deputy Paulsen of my honorary deputy status." I offer him a smug grin and arch one eyebrow before continuing. "Obvious signs of a struggle. I'm sure the medical examiner will find a few interesting things under Tanya's fingernails. Was she in some kind of trouble? She was the best dry cleaner in Birch County. I can't imagine anyone killing her over a stain she couldn't remove."

My psychic senses happily acknowledge Erick's weakening resolve. "Look, Moon, this case could be more dangerous than it seems. It could be a random homicide committed by an interrupted burglar, but Tanya has made a few enemies over the years. She's extremely outspoken and takes action on her beliefs. Not everyone appreciates that. I have Deputy Johnson looking into the various organizations she belonged to or supported." He exhales in frustration, leans closer, and lowers his voice to barely a whisper. "Is her ghost still around? Are you getting any of your, you know, psychic flashes?"

His blustery public speech was meant for others, but I plan to let him stew a little before I cave. "Interesting. First, I'm *persona non grata*, and now you're pumping me for information like a circus sideshow freak. Which is it, Sheriff?"

Erick removes his latex gloves, tucks them in a

pocket, and slips a hand under my elbow as he gently escorts me through the back door of the cleaners. Once we're away from prying eyes and ears, he relents. "You know how much I appreciate your help. But the election is only a few months behind us, and Paulsen is still stinging from the loss. I don't need to give her any reasons to call for a recount."

My jaw drops open like the rear cargo door on a C-130. "What are you saying? Are you accusing me of being a threat to your employment? I don't think solving cases and putting murderers in jail is a bad thing, Sheriff."

His head tilts from right shoulder to left shoulder. He rakes a hand through his blond hair and smooths a loose swath of bangs back into the pomade. "Like I said, I always appreciate your help. I think you just need to back off a bit. Call me with your insights rather than dropping in. It's completely against protocol to have civilians at a crime scene." He offers a placating smile and bobs his head in a way that seems like he's doffing a cap. "Let us do our job, Mitzy. I'll send a copy of the report to your lawyer, and if you happen to overhear an interrogation or two while you're patiently waiting for me in my office, there's not much I can do about that. I'd appreciate it if you'd head back to the bookshop. You understand, don't you?"

Placing a fist on my ample hip, I fix Erick with an unwavering stare. "What I don't understand is what I'm supposed to do with this Vera Wang dress? Tanya is the only person Grams trusts with her couture."

Erick's cheeks flush, and he glances hastily left and right to make sure no one overheard me mentioning my dearly departed grandmother as though she still exists. Of course, between you and me, she does. As you know, her ghost happily resides in my bookshop, and we have a wonderful relationship — which at long last, Erick knows about. Although he's eager for me to keep it all on the DL.

"I'm sure there's a decent dry cleaner in Broken Rock or Grand Falls. You could also wait until we finish the investigation. Tanya's wife will have everything back up and running in a couple weeks."

I shrug noncommittally.

He slips an arm around my waist and kisses me on the cheek. "Can I walk you home?"

Pulling back, I scoff openly. "Hardly. I bundled up and mustered the courage to leave my house in this weather. There's no way I'm going back home without some food. I'll walk through the alley and grab some lunch at the diner. Will I see you later tonight?"

Sheriff Harper grins foolishly and winks. "Absolutely."

And now my tummy tingles in an entirely more delicious way.

Hurrying back to Main Street, I burst into Myrtle's Diner, stomp the slushy mess off my boots, and shiver as the inviting warmth reaffirms how cold it was outside.

My grandfather, Odell Johnson, offers me a spatula salute through the red-Formica-trimmed orders-up window. I unzip my jacket but leave it on for the time being, and slide onto a red-vinyl bench seat.

The world's kindest, most efficient waitress is only a step behind. Tally places a steaming mug of java onto the silver-flecked white Formica table and winks. "Looks like you heard."

My face shifts from blank to confused in the blink of an eye. "Heard what?"

She points to the crumpled dress sharing my bench seat. "Oh, I assumed . . . Because of the dress . . ."

"Oh, right. I did hear about Tanya. I just came from the dry cleaner. But you already guessed that." Taking a sip of coffee to buy myself some time and steady my nerves, I offer her the only information I have. "I got kicked out of the crime scene. Nothing to share . . . Poor Tanya."

Tally nods her flame-red bun and hurries off to refill coffees for the two locals seated at the counter.

CHAPTER 3

Entering my bookshop through the less glamorous metal door in the alleyway, I tiptoe past the back room and successfully avoid any embarrassing interaction with my hyper-vigilant employee, Twiggy.

Lucky for me, I successfully negotiate the chain and the circular staircase. Grabbing the candle sconce next to my copy of *Saducismus Triumphatus,* I tilt it downward and activate the secret bookcase door. As soon as it slides open, I rush into the apartment. "Grams? Grams! We have to set up the murder wall."

To be fair, our wall is actually more of a rolling corkboard since someone (Twiggy) specifically forbade me from putting any tacks into the original lath and plaster walls. Also, I'm forced to use green yarn to signify connections between the victim and the suspects due to the fact that red yarn gives our resident ghost the heebie-jeebies.

Normally, Grams pops into existence a moment after I utter the call. This time there's a significant delay. I wasn't gifted with patience, so I head directly for the stack of 3 x 5 cards on the coffee table and grab the pen.

Before I can scratch a single letter onto the cardstock, Myrtle Isadora blasts through the wall. "Mitzy! Don't you dare steal my one and only job!"

The truth of that statement tickles my funny bone, and I laugh until little tears leak from the corners of my eyes. "Truer words were never spoken. Did you ever have a job?"

"Oh, sweetie! Don't be ridiculous. Raising a family is a job. Serving on the boards of several charitable organizations and planning elaborate fundraisers is a job. And let's not forget, I ran this bookstore."

"Come on, Grams. You and I both know Twiggy ran the bookstore. And raising one child, while I'm sure challenging, is a generous use of the word family."

"Mizithra! You know for a fact that your father was an incredible handful."

"Runs in the family, I suppose."

"Well, I never!"

"I think it's fair to say you did, at least five times, Myrtle Isadora Johnson Linder Duncan Willamet Rogers."

The familiar refrain breaks the tension, and we share a chuckle.

"You only left the house ten minutes ago. How on earth did you find a —?" Her eyes fall on the crumpled Vera Wang tossed recklessly on the over-stuffed settee. "No!"

"I'm sorry, Grams. The victim is Tanya. Erick kicked me out of the crime scene with zero information. All I could tell from my short time in the cleaners was that she was suffocated — or strangled — and she put up quite a fight."

"I should think so! That woman was the inspiration for *Erin Brockovich.*"

"Hold on. My movie knowledge is pretty extensive. That's not right."

She crosses her arms and pouts. "I was speaking metaphorically."

"I'm not exactly sure you know what a metaphor is, Grams. Plus, I'm having a hard time understanding how a local dry cleaner could be the inspiration for the lawyer/activist character in a major motion picture."

The smug grin that spreads across her ethereal face is unnerving. "Well, I guess you don't know as much as you think you do, Miss Smarty-Pants."

"Touché. What am I missing?"

Grams writes a card for Tanya and floats it over to the corkboard.

Taking the card, I tack it firmly in the center. As I turn away, something catches my eye. "Tanya Tucker? Her name was actually Tanya Tucker, like the famous country singer?"

Grams shrugs her designer-gown-clad shoulders. "I can't say I've ever heard of that singer, dear. I'll take your word for it."

Oh brother. "So, Erick mentioned there was a lot I didn't know about Tanya, and you brought it to my attention that she's some kind of inspiration for the Erin Brockovich character. Can you elaborate?"

Grams crosses her arms, purses her lips, and tilts her head insistently.

Without her having to say a word, I know what she's thinking. *You get more flies with honey.* "Would you *please* share what you know, dearest Grand-ma-ma?"

My teasing brings a smile to Isadora's shimmering face. "I have no idea what she's gotten into lately, but when I was alive, Tanya had a habit of representing the underdogs. She went to law school and passed the bar, but before she could set up her own practice, she decided being a full-time, cut-throat lawyer wasn't for her."

The hairs on the back of my neck tingle, and the

cantankerous mood ring on my left hand forms an icy chill around my finger. "There's something you're not telling me, Isadora." My extrasensory perceptions are buzzing with hidden secrets.

"Oh, Mitzy. It's such a sad story. Tanya really was immensely talented and had such a generous heart. The problem was, that kindhearted attitude sent her to the defense side of the courtroom. She had a few small misdemeanor cases, but her first big case was a murder."

My audible gasp interrupts her flow.

"Well, everyone in town swore the man was guilty, but somehow Tanya got him off on a technicality. At first, she was pleased, and the success bolstered her courage." Grams squeezes her eyelids shut, and I know there's no happy ending,

"About ten days later, he was involved in a domestic dispute that resulted in three deaths. Tanya was never the same. She quit lawyering, bought the dry cleaners, married Pilar, and settled down."

Tears spring to my eyes. "How awful for her. The murder part, not the other stuff."

Ghost-ma nods wistfully. "They eventually adopted two wonderful children, and Tanya never looked back. Her tendency to root for the underdog, however, never fully disappeared. She kept her licenses up to date and offered her services pro bono to a number of charitable organizations. The animal shelter, a battered-women's shelter, and a few women's sporting leagues."

"Are you saying somehow her involvement in charity work got her murdered?"

"Well, the women's wrestling group did tend to attract a rough-and-tumble kind of gal. I'm sure there's a backstory or two worth investigating there, and we've all heard terrible stories of abusive ex-husbands desperate to find the secret location of the women's shelter. I know Tanya would never give anyone up without a fight."

A heavy weight presses my shoulders down. "You're definitely right about that. She fought like heck." Dropping onto the overstuffed settee, I let the information my grandmother shared trickle through my brain like beads in a rainstick. It's a whole Sedona, woo woo reference. Not important.

"Let's make out a card for any organizations that you're aware of, and I'll see if I can have a friendly chat with Pilar."

Ghost-ma presses a shimmering hand to her chest and sighs dramatically. "Pilar must be devastated. They were so happy together and such wonderful parents."

"Would Odell know how to get hold of her? Or Twiggy?"

Grams' aura glows so brightly I have to shield

my eyes. "Oh, Twiggy can make the introductions. She and Tanya went to high school together."

"Hopefully, I won't have to bargain away my soul for the favor." We share a chuckle at Twiggy's expense.

Based on the strange grey clouds stewing over the great lake nestled in the harbor behind my book-shop, I grab a raincoat rather than a puffy jacket and head downstairs to see if Twiggy will play nice.

When I walk into the back room, she slowly turns to face me. I can't help myself. Every time she spins around in that dilapidated office chair, shades of Dr. Evil come to mind.

"Who put the bee in your bonnet this time, kid?"

"No bees, and not my bonnet this time. Unfortunately, someone killed Tanya, and —"

Twiggy is on her feet in a heartbeat. "What are you talking about? When did this happen? Who's responsible? I'll set them straight."

Taking a deep breath, I allow her questions to hang in the air for a moment before giving her the information I possess. "So, I was hoping you could make an introduction to Pilar and see if she'd be willing to talk to me. I need way more information about the work Tanya was doing outside the dry cleaners to have any chance of solving this one."

"So, Mitzy Moon is on the case?"

"As Pyewacket would say, can confirm."

Twiggy cackles briefly at my reference to the almost-human mascot of our bookstore. "Let me make a quick phone call, doll. Sit tight."

Another one of my least favorite phrases. I've never sat tight a day in my life, and I don't plan on starting now. As I shift my weight impatiently from left foot to right, Twiggy finally finishes her call.

"It's a good news, bad news situation. Pilar wants to help, but she's a wreck."

"Well, I'm no therapist, but I've got some experience with crushing loss. I can handle uncomfortable situations."

My volunteer employee gets to her feet, smooths her dungarees, and stomps her biker-boot-clad feet closer. "That's what I like about you, kid. You're no starry-eyed damsel in distress. You get things done." She hands me a slip of paper with an address and some bare-bones directions, and pats me on the shoulder as I head out the side door beneath the glowing red "Exit" sign.

Let's hope I can get this thing done.

CHAPTER 4

I learned the hard way that GPS can be spotty, at best, in almost-Canada, so it's prudent to take a minute to familiarize myself with the chicken-scratch directions and then back my Jeep out of the garage.

Pilar and Tanya's place is in an unfamiliar part of town, but nowhere near as hard to find as Silas Willoughby's strange Gothic mansion.

A brightly painted mailbox and several elaborate children's toys clearly mark the home I'm searching for.

Easing into the short driveway, I practice one of my strategies to make sure I've opened up my psychic abilities. Silas has taught me so many things, but learning how to protect myself when necessary or switch my abilities on full whack when needed is probably the most useful.

My extrasensory perceptions span the range from clairsentience, clairaudience, clairvoyance, all the way to claircognizance. So if I leave myself wide open 24/7, it's a good way to get a headache or worse. Going into this meeting, I definitely want everything on high alert. In my experience, the bereaved may hide things for a number of reasons. Not the least of which is simply being overwhelmed.

Carefully latching the sturdy wooden gate behind me, I walk up the concrete steps and knock on the storm door.

A petite brunette with her hair pulled back in a ponytail, and red-rimmed eyes, opens the door. "Mitzy Moon?"

"Yes. You must be Pilar. I'm so sorry for — everything. I hope there's some way I can help. Thank you for agreeing to talk to me."

Fresh tears roll down her cheeks as she ushers me into their cozy living room. Toys, games, and books all neatly line a set of low shelves.

"Are the children home?"

She glances up at me, clenches her jaw, and shakes her head. "I had to send them over to our friends. I didn't want them to see me —" Another batch of salty tears burst from her eyes and sobs shake her shoulders.

I move closer to her on the sofa and place a comforting arm around her shoulders. "I know you don't know me, but I'm all-too-familiar with loss. My mother was tragically taken from me when I was eleven. You may not want comfort from basically a stranger, but I'm here. You can say anything."

Pilar leans into me and unabashedly cries for several minutes.

Eventually, she catches her breath and exhales raggedly. "Thank you. It's all so raw. I don't even want to believe it's true. I have no idea what I'm going to tell the children."

"Speaking from experience, you need to tell them the truth. An age-appropriate version, but it has to be the truth. They need to grieve, just like you. If you keep the truth from them, they won't be able to process things — or heal."

She reaches out and grips my left hand tightly. "Thank you. You're so right. My grandmother passed away when I was nine, and my mother made up a foolish story about a nursing home too far away to visit . . . Looking back, it seems absolutely insane. I didn't find out my grandmother had passed away until five years later when a cousin made a comment at Christmas. I was devastated. My mother didn't even give me the closure of attending a funeral." She pauses, temporarily pulls the scrunchy from her hair, and quickly scrapes her hair back into a new pony. "Anyway, I can deal with all of that later. Twiggy said it would be helpful for you to know some things about Tanya's work. Like what?"

"Right. Twiggy mentioned that Tanya kept working as a lawyer, pro bono. I understand she worked with the animal shelter, the battered-women's shelter, and some women's wrestling thing?"

Pilar nods. "There are a few smaller organizations, but those three took up most of her time. Her clients love . . . loved her. She was their champion. Even some of the ex-con gals in the wrestling league never spoke a bad word about Tanya."

I attempt to keep my outside calm, but the mention of "ex-cons" makes the hair on the back of my neck stand on end. That's something to make a note of. I happen to know more than my share about the topic. My ex-con father runs a restorative justice program helping former felons find jobs and integrate back into society. I've seen the positive realities of rehabilitation, but I'm more concerned with the people who don't rehabilitate. "Did she have any clients who dropped out of the program?

Maybe a wife or girlfriend who returned to an abusive relationship?"

"There were a few who struggled with independence. But returning definitely wouldn't have gotten Tanya in any trouble. It was the aggressive husbands' demanding information that could be the real problem."

"All right. Let's start there. Did she mention anything about a confrontation recently?"

Pilar shakes her head. "No. But that doesn't necessarily mean nothing was happening. We make a point of not discussing those things in front of the children. And when you have two children under twelve, you're almost always in front of the children." A brief smile lifts her mouth before she remembers the tragedy of the day.

"Makes sense. What about the wrestling business? Was there a rival league, or protesters, or maybe a bad-seed wrestler?" My left hand is unconsciously rubbing the engagement ring on my right ring finger. The ring is new to me, but I like the comfort of its history with Grams and Odell. Yes, most girls wear their engagement ring on the left hand, but a slightly magical and very moody mood ring — that insists on staying exactly where it's at — occupies that ring finger. If I hope to continue receiving helpful visions or tidbits of information, I best leave well enough alone. My gesture draws Pilar's attention.

"Is that your engagement ring?"

A self-conscious flush rushes to my cheeks. "Sorry. It's all so new, I forget I'm even doing that."

A wave of distrust rolls toward me. "I mentioned it to Twiggy, but I'll say it again. Some of the women in the shelter and some women who wrestle have 'a past.' They're working hard to change and give themselves a fresh start. It wouldn't benefit them to fall into the crosshairs of law enforcement."

"I absolutely understand. I know Sheriff Harper will prioritize the current investigation and not nitpick about past indiscretions. Is there any chance I could speak to some of the women directly?"

Pilar rockets to her feet and paces across the area rug. "Absolutely not. As far as the shelter is concerned, those women are off-limits. And the wrestlers . . . Well, they're a super tightknit group. Instantly suspicious of outsiders."

An idea bubbles to the surface, and a smile brightens my features. "I grew up in the foster system, Pilar. I'm not proud of it, but I got into more than my share of scraps. What if I join the team, you know, undercover? I could have a false identity and everything. That way, I could blend in as one of them and look around for information when opportunities present themselves."

Pilar twists her hands back and forth in front of her and bites her lower lip.

I swear, I can sense her heart rate increasing.

Hopefully, I can push her past this hesitation. "Again, I wouldn't be there to out anyone. I'd be there to get information about who murdered your wife." It's difficult for me to be so blunt, but I need her to understand what we're dealing with. If I can't get in front of these women, I can't use my extrasensory perceptions to ferret out the truth.

Pilar groans and rubs her hands across her face. "You're right. I owe it to Tanya to make this happen. And you're also right about undercover being the best solution. Are you sure you can handle it? I would feel terrible if you got seriously injured."

"Seriously injured? Wrestling is mostly play-acting and props, right?"

Pilar's deep-brown eyes widen. "Oh no. Everything is exaggerated, but there's plenty of good, old-fashioned pain. If you're going to do this, you better be prepared to get more than your share of bumps and bruises."

Well, looks like I've gotten myself in over my head once again. "Sounds great. Just let me know where and when to show up."

"I'll text you the details." Pilar hands me her

phone and I input my contact info. As I hand it back, she fixes me with a concerned stare. "You'll need to work on your character. The gals will be suspicious if you show up and don't have a solid thing."

"Thing?" I scrunch up my face and tilt my head.

She pulls air between her teeth and hums. "Well, maybe an example will help. One gal is named Candy Cornwell. Her character is from a farm in Nebraska that used to raise the best corn in the country. Then some big bad developer stole her family's land, and she wrestles to earn money to buy back their farm."

"Yeesh! That's so detailed. I need to give this some serious thought."

"Yeah. And you need a signature move."

"A what?" My eyebrows feel like they might fly off my forehead.

"Candy Cornwell's signature takedown move is the 'crusher.' It's a little derivative, but fans love it when she leaps off the top rope and flattens her opponent."

My throat is getting dry, and I can't seem to swallow. I may have legitimately bitten off more than even I can chew. Too late to back out now. "All right. I'll get to work. Go team!"

Pilar struggles to smile and nod.

With that, I offer her one last comforting hug and head back to Pin Cherry.

I'm not sure whether Grams is going to be excited or furious about putting together my wrestling costume!

CHAPTER 5

Tiptoeing past the back room, I attempt to channel the stealth of Pyewacket as I sneak up to the apartment.

If Twiggy gets even a whiff of this, she'll cackle herself into a coma.

Normally, Grams would be tucked away on the third floor of the printing museum, working on her "memoirs," which turned out to be all about me. However, since we donated all the historical artifacts to an international printing museum on the West Coast and started the renovations on a three-story walkup, she's been working at a small desk in my apartment.

Reaching up, I pull the candle handle, and as the secret bookcase door slides open, two heads whip-pan from the computer screen to my concerned face. Both the ghost eyes and the cat eyes are brimming with guilt.

"What exactly are you two getting into?" If it were only Ghost-ma, I'd assume she was watching the infamous proposal video for the eleven millionth time, but with Pyewacket assisting her, I suspect the worst.

Pyewacket slams his paw on the keyboard and leaps to the heights of safety atop an antique armoire.

Grams instantly floats toward the ceiling. "Have you had a look across the lake? I think it's really beginning to thaw. Aren't you looking forward to the warmer weather?"

"All right, you two. What on earth are you attempting to buy? I think we're going to have to put some spending limits on your new online shopping pastime." Pin Cherry is famously the town that tech forgot, but I had to install a special computer for video conferencing with my feline/ghost support team when I took an out-of-town case. It seems I'll live to regret that upgrade. Their recent foray into the interweb is becoming dangerous.

Grams' ethereal hand gently touches the side of her pseudo-innocent face. "Let's not get carried away, sweetie. Try to remember where your large inheritance came from."

"Oh, is that the game we're playing? I'd like the

record to reflect that you passed your estate on to me — officially — when you passed from this plane to whatever in-between place you currently reside." She opens her mouth, but I point a warning finger in her direction and continue. "Keep in mind that I'm not selfishly hoarding the money like Scrooge McDuck. I run a generous philanthropic organization that gives back to our community. And let's not forget the winter sports arena that Dad and I recently rebuilt."

In the face of my selfless generosity, Grams relents. "Oh, I suppose you're right, dear. I just want everything to be absolutely perfect for the wedding."

In retrospect, giving her carte blanche with the wedding planning may have been a mistake. "I appreciate the effort, Isadora, but you know Erick and I want to keep things simple. We're happy to be marrying each other. That's enough. I know you want everything to be over-the-top and larger-than-life, but can you try to keep things partially grounded in reality?"

"I'll try, dear. But you are my only granddaughter, and you know how much I love planning a wedding."

"Boy, do I! Five and counting! Myrtle Isadora Johnson Linder Duncan Willamet Rogers."

Grams and I share a giggle that ends in a ghost

snort, and Pyewacket lazily leaps down, sensing the coast is clear.

"Not so fast, Mr. Cuddlekins. Grams is gonna need a sponsor if she's officially going to kick the online shopping habit. I'm holding you responsible since you seem to be the enabler."

"RE-OW!" Game on!

"I hope that means I can count on you to be levelheaded in the future. Correct?"

"Reow." Can confirm.

The negotiation is over, and I can finally share my big news.

Ghost-ma rockets from the ceiling and stops barely an inch from my nose. "Big news? What big news?"

Pointing an irritated finger toward my lips, I shake my head once. She knows the signal for no thought-dropping. Since she never pays attention to the signal, simply thinking this retribution is enough.

Once again, she casts her gaze toward the harbor and inhales sharply.

My limited patience has run out. "I'm going undercover."

Those three little words get her every time. Before I explain a single detail of my mission, she zooms into the closet and begins questioning me like a KGB agent. "What's your back story? Are you blending in or standing out? Hair color could be important. Sexy or subdued?"

Walking through the doorway, I calmly take a seat on the padded mahogany bench in the center of this seemingly endless wardrobe warehouse and casually examine my fingernails, thrilled at the building suspense.

"Oh, Mitzy! Now you're just being cruel. Spill."

"I'm joining the women's wrestling league." My throat tightens as I await her reaction.

There's a gasp, a giggle, and then mad swirling. "Fantastic! You know I did a little roller derby in my time. There was no women's wrestling league back then. How exciting! I think I have a leopard-print catsuit in here somewhere . . ." She rifles through the hangers with gentle intensity.

"Look, I don't mean to be *this* girl, but I don't really see myself in head-to-toe spandex. You know what I mean?"

Grams pauses her search, rotates, and scans me from head to toe. "I think your natural snow-white hair will be fantastic. It will stand out. Plus, you have a well-rounded backside and a decent rack."

"Grams! Rude!"

"Nonsense." She waves away my protest. "There's absolutely nothing wrong with a woman taking stock of her assets."

Since she mentioned my backside and has now used the word "assets," I giggle like a schoolgirl.

"Oh dear. You know what I mean."

"I guess . . . I need to come up with a character name, a backstory, and a signature move. It's a lot."

She circles the mahogany bench, and her gaze drifts away as she creates this character.

"I'm thinking hometown hero. Something with cherry in the name." She grabs a white button-down blouse with a field of cherries printed across the fabric. "You can tie this up like what's her name on that TV show about those hicks moving to Beverly Hills."

"Are you talking about Elly May from *The Beverly Hillbillies*?" I can see Elly's little gingham top knotted underneath her tatas and the thought of exposing that much skin does not delight.

"Look, sweetie, you're too nice to play a heel. That's what they call the villains. You've got to go the babyface route, and the audience wants a show. Play to your strengths." She returns to wardrobe prep. "Now, if we match that with a nice pair of denim cutoffs —"

"Wait. Am I Elly May or Daisy Duke?"

Ghost-ma's smile lights up the whole closet. "Yes! Exactly." She rifles through a drawer, throws the denim shorts at me, and crosses her arms. "Try them on! I have to see you in character to get my inspiration."

Blerg.

It's fruitless to argue with my bossy phantom. I strip down to my chonies and put on the ridiculously short shorts. As I'm attempting to knot the shirt as low as possible, Grams finds enough corporeal strength to yank the knot up at least three inches.

"There. That's perfect. You already look the part. Ooooh! Pigtails!" She vanishes through the wall into the adjacent bathroom and shouts for me to follow.

I walk around to the doorway like a civilized human.

She scrapes my hair into two high pigtails and rummages through the drawers in search of something she calls cutie-pie ribbons.

No idea.

"We'll have to get ribbons. It's probably too late to run over to Rex's Drugstore, but you can grab them first thing tomorrow morning before you head to practice, or rehearsal, or whatever they call it."

"I don't know what they call it, Grams. And I'm waiting for a text from Pilar to get the details on when and where they practice." Glancing at myself in the mirror, I can't help but giggle yet again. "Are you serious with this? I feel ridiculous."

She gazes at my reflection and beams with pride. "Cherry Sundae. No, that's not it. Cherry Jubilee. No, not quite . . ."

Turning away from my reflection, I offer my aid. "Maybe if we come up with my signature move, that will help us with the name?"

She taps a finger on her lips and nods. "Yes. Good idea. What can you do?"

"Um. I honestly don't know that much about professional wrestling. But my foster brother Jarrell taught me a sleeper hold thingy. He said it was the best way to give yourself time to get away."

My grandmother's glowing eyes widen, and her brows arch severely. "I hope I never have the displeasure of meeting this Jarrell. I blame him for most of your miscreant deeds."

"Hey now. Give me some credit. I would've gotten into trouble no matter what. Let's all remember which family tree I dropped from."

Grams recoils and then guffaws. "I suppose you're right, dear." Once again, her aura brightens. "Cherry Choker!"

I groan. "Seems a little too on the nose."

"I think it's perfect. We have choke cherries as well as pin cherries all over this county. What do you have?"

"Cherry Chip? Cherry Chupacabra?"

She squeals with laughter. "I think it's going to

have to be Cherry Choker, sweetie. With a signature move like the sleeper, it just seems to fit."

"Fine. Put a pin in it, and let's see if we can find some different shorts." Looking over my shoulder into the mirror, I can see entirely too much of my own assets.

Grams chuckles. "I've seen the costumes, sweetie. What you've got on may already be too tame. You'll be lucky if they don't toss you into a bikini top!"

All the color drains from my face and I struggle to swallow.

What have I done?

CHAPTER 6

ARMED WITH NOTHING more than a pair of used wrestling boots and an informational text from Pilar, I head over to a rented exhibition hall at the county fairgrounds miles outside of town. I've been here once before for a best-pie contest, but that's another story.

In the off-season, the grounds are thick with snow-covered dead weeds and thin on humans, so it doesn't take long to locate the league's building. As predicted, the women stretching, jumping, and hefting various weights or medicine balls are all in their working wardrobes.

The scent in the air is an odd combination of perspiration and hope.

Peeling off my warm coat, I can't say I'm actually happy to be in cutoffs and a ridiculously knotted blouse, but when I catch sight of Pilar, a flash of relief sparks through my chest.

"Who's the fresh meat?" a broad-shouldered giant of a woman bellows as I approach.

Pilar gestures for the women to settle down and take their seats on the temporary bleachers.

After a deep, steadying breath, I walk toward her and prepare for the worst.

"Ladies, I'm sure you've all heard about the terrible tragedy that struck our family."

An interesting mix of confusion, condolences, and threatening grumbles ripples through the crowd of wrestlers.

"The sheriff is looking into things, and I know he'll solve this terrible —" her voice catches and she pauses to gather the strength to continue "— this heinous crime as quickly as possible." Pilar tucks her hair behind her ear and struggles to keep back tears.

"I'll have to step away from the day-to-day of coaching — Someone has to keep the dry cleaners running. Since Anna Mel Cracker is our most experienced wrestler, she'll be taking over coaching duties for the foreseeable future."

A tall woman of girth, dressed in a circus ringmaster outfit, nods in agreement and cracks her whip.

"I'll work on finding a lawyer who's willing to

pick up the fight where Tanya left off." Pilar continues, "And we're adding a new gal to the roster as well."

All eyes lock on me. To be clear, there's no general air of welcome. The faces range from suspicious to malicious.

Pilar whispers, "Introduce yourself."

Taking a deep breath, I prepare to launch into my best Southern accent. "Hey, I'm Cherry Darling." Their murmurs of approval confirm my last-minute name change was inspiration itself. "I just got off the bus from Texas, and I'm looking for a fresh start. My mama died in a cattle drive accident, and my pa . . . Well, I'd rather not say. I'm here to make my own way in the world, and hope to give as good as I get." With my ending phrase, I stomp my foot and place a hand on my hip.

A faint chuckle drifts my way as a woman dressed in drab colors and wearing a grey fur ushanka gets to her feet. In a thick Russian accent, she gives me the lay of the land. "I am Ivana Vodka. You will find no easy way to the top. You work hard. If good, maybe you survive." She sits down, and I take that to signal the end of her welcome speech.

The next gal to jump to her feet walks toward me and offers her hand. I reach out to shake it, but she grips my arm and flips me onto my back in the blink of an eye. As cartoon stars circle my head, I gaze upward, blinking against the flickering fluorescent lights.

"Hey, Hallucna Jenn here." She somehow makes a tattered straightjacket look sexy. "I'm never who you think I am. I'm never predictable."

Hallucna Jenn returns to her seat as a large golden-haired girl walks toward me, reaches down, and pulls me to my feet. Her solid strength makes me seem light as a feather. "Candy Cornwell. Don't let these guys psych you out. We're always happy to have another wrestler in the league. You'll get the hang of it. As long as you don't cross Anita Gurney."

A woman dressed in a bloody paramedic's shirt, and shorts nearly as tiny as mine, growls, but then offers a wink.

Must be Anita Gurney. Cool name.

The play on words brings a chuckle, and laughter eases the tension in the room.

Anna Mel Cracker expertly rolls under the bottom rope and hops to her feet in the squared circle. "Get in here, Cherry." She gestures to a post-apocalyptic punk rocker in the front row. "Rita Riot, you're gonna be her first opponent. Obviously, Cherry is a babyface. Play into that, Cherry. The rubes love a hero. Get the crowd on your side. And then show us your move."

Anna Mel bounces out of the ring, and Rita

Riot, sporting a torn T-shirt and Mad Max-esque shoulder pads, quickly climbs in and replaces her. Without so much as an introduction or a bow, she runs for the ropes behind me, whoops with dastardly pleasure, and races toward the ropes on the other side. As she bounces back, an image of an old clothesline maneuver pops into my head, giving me just enough time to duck beneath the spot where her steel arm would've made impact with my throat.

Her powerful forearm brushes across the tops of the little white pigtails bouncing on my head.

That was too close.

The other wrestlers cheer, and someone yells, "Good job, Cherry!"

My extrasensory abilities may give me just the advantage I need in this unpredictable sport. As I turn to prepare for her next advance, she circles me, looking for purchase.

I hear the word "airplane" floating through the ether and realize she's planning to hoist me into the air and spin me.

Two things that should prevent that: my quick footwork, and my not inconsiderable weight.

Dodging the move, I duck behind her, spin, and hook my right arm under her chin. Pressing my left arm over the right for leverage, I slowly squeeze. I'm able to put her to *sleep* within seconds.

Rita falls limp in my arms.

I release her and throw my hands in the air. Her body hits the mat with a thud of finality, and most of the women get to their feet and cheer. Not too bad for my first match.

Wouldn't it be nice if I could say I exited the ring with grace? We all know that's not my style. I get all wadded up in the ropes and leave the squared circle in a dumpster fire of tripping, bouncing, and gasping.

As I reach the bleachers and take a seat next to the rest of the team, Rita sits up on the canvas and rubs her neck. "That was for real, gals. There was no communication, and I didn't take a fall. Cherry seriously put the choker on me and my lights went out." Rita jumps to her feet and stretches her neck from side to side. "I'm a little salty about that, Cherry. Good storyline for the next card."

Rather than upset, I sense respect as she exits the ring and returns to the bleachers.

Pilar asks everyone to take a moment of silence for Tanya and promises to keep us all updated on the investigation.

Now that I've passed the hazing, hopefully, I can ask a few questions without anyone getting too suspicious.

The rest of practice is less about grandstanding and way more about communication.

These women take their sport seriously, and the difference between putting on a good show and putting someone in the hospital is the razor's edge.

Anna Mel spends a few quality moments with me, one-on-one. "Thing is, Cherry, we expect to get knocked down. Bumps and bruises, even the occasional sprain, are par for the course. What we want to avoid is any injury that puts a wrestler out for a paid spot on the next card, or, worse, a career-ender."

Sticking to my Southern roots, I reply, "Gotcha. Was that wrong of me to put the choker hold —"

"Never question your instincts. One thing I can tell about you, you got good instincts. That's a great signature move, and I wouldn't change a thing. I'm talking about the big stuff. Pile drivers, clotheslines, figure-four leg locks . . . You know, the more dangerous moves. A lot of these gals are bigger than you, and they will automatically go for submission holds if you give 'em the opportunity. You have to be one step ahead."

"Clear as the mornin' dew — now!" Looks like my extrasensory abilities are going to play a huge part in Cherry Darling's rise to fame.

Anna Mel heads off to work with other wrestlers, and I absently grab a couple of dumbbells to do some bicep curls. Never having been an actual gym rat, I only remember a few exercises they forced me to perform back in high school phys-ed class. Hopefully, practice will end soon.

Rita Riot approaches with her hands comically held high. "Take it easy on me, Cherry. I only want to talk."

Chuckling, I hang my head. "Dagnabbit! I'm awful sorry about that. I wasn't tryin' to show off or anything."

She slips an arm around my shoulders and squeezes hard. "Don't put yourself down. We support each other here. Everyone gets a chance in the spotlight. Even the heels. Every good wrestling story-line has a heel the audience loves to hate and a babyface the audience loves to love. Doesn't matter so much who wins or loses, as long as the narrative is believable. Heels have fans too."

"So I'm a babyface, one of the good guys."

"Good *gals*. Not to be all feminist, or whatevs. But around here, girl power is queen."

"Gotcha."

"We don't have a locker room or anything here, so everybody shows up in their gear. Some of us bring a change of clothes and grab a drink after practice. Maybe next time you can join us?"

"That's right kind of ya."

As Rita walks back to the main group, a strange thought penetrates my consciousness. I'm not all that used to being in a group of females that support each other unquestioningly. No wonder Tanya was drawn to their cause. Which, by the way, I need to find out more about. Change of clothes or not, I need to invite myself to *this* after-practice drinks sesh.

CHAPTER 7

Promising to keep my coat on, covering my costume, while inside the establishment, I follow the short caravan to a dive bar I've never heard of in the nearby town of Broken Rock.

The Plucked Chicken lives up to its name. Why does that *not* surprise me?

An old barn has been converted into a resto-pub. I use that term loosely. Inside, the décor leans heavily into the poultry theme. An eight-foot, neon-enhanced rooster illuminates the far corner while hens and eggs of all shapes, sizes, and materials leer down from dusty walls and rafters.

A server wearing a "Wet Your Beak!" T-shirt invites us to order at the bar and find a seat "anywhere we like."

There's even a specialty "COCK-tail" menu. I will spare you the pun-laden drink names. The food offerings consist entirely of chicken- and chicken-wing-related dishes. The bar also features a few local brews on tap and severely limited options for hard liquor.

Keeping my cards close to the vest, I restrain myself from offering to buy everyone a round. I should probably continue to play a struggling escapee from Texas. My character's backstory may as well be tied closely to my cover story.

Everyone grabs a beverage and gravitates toward a large corner booth. The initial talk is all about what went right or wrong in practice and how things can be refined for the big title match on Saturday.

"Cherry? Did Pilar tell you if you're on the card?"

Not knowing precisely what a card is, I shrug.

Rita pipes up. "She'll totally be on the card. Not like the title match or anything, but definitely the second or third slot. We absolutely need a new hero."

A flash of offense works its way across Anna Mel's face. She doesn't offer any verbal response, but it's clear that she fancies herself the main attraction.

Good to know.

"Hey, not to be the ranch hand with no gloves or anything, but what was all that stuff about Tanya?"

Five heads swivel toward me in a united expression. Suspicion.

"Beggin' y'all's pardon. Don't even answer that. Where are my manners?" I pretend to look under the table and smile sheepishly. "It's just the way Pilar was talkin', and the moment of silence —" My Texas-sized accent and my resolve waver.

Rita reaches out and grabs Candy Cornwell's large hand. "I think we should tell her. She's one of us now."

Candy nods, but withdraws her hand from the Riot's grasp.

Rita glances once around the table for any objection and dives in. "Tanya is Pilar's wife. They run a dry-cleaning business together in Pin Cherry Harbor. But Tanya's also our lawyer. The men's wrestling league has been giving us a heckuva time. Their general manager doesn't think there's room for the both of us."

Anna Mel jumps in. "He doesn't seem to understand how audience building works. The guy thinks if we're all on the card, that'll somehow split the audience. Has some nonsense theory that people who love wrestling only love watching men wrestle. He's an idiot!" Her fist slams down on the table. The glasses hop and ice clinks.

"Gotcha. So this guy stirred up a hornet's nest of trouble with Tanya?"

Rita puts her hand over her mouth and shakes her head. Candy tags in. "Tanya was murdered. Yesterday."

Hoping my acting skills are better than usual, I open my eyes and mouth wide. "Dear Lord baby Jesus. I'm right sorry. I never would've —"

Rita nods and pats my arm. "It's okay. You had no way of knowing."

Candy continues. "Tanya is the most honorable person you'll ever meet. She worked super hard for us, and we could no way afford to pay her. But if it wasn't for her legal stuff, that weasel Dylan Bernard would've already pushed one of his injunctions through. It's like it's his life's mission to make women's wrestling disappear from the face of the earth."

Taking what I feel is a lengthy enough beat, I dive in. "You don't reckon he had somethin' to do with Tanya's murder, do you?"

Four of the heads nod fervently. Only Rita abstains. "We can't be sure. He's conniving and soulless, but I'm not sure he's homicidal."

As the table grumbles out the pros and cons of Dylan's guilt or innocence, I let my wheels turn. It might be best to quit while I'm ahead, excuse myself, and get home to update the murder wall. Any additional pushing is going to seem too suspicious.

Knocking back the last of my *Witch's Tart* cider, I slide out of the booth and smile warmly. "I gotta hustle on home and feed my cat. But thanks y'all, for makin' me feel welcome as a second cousin. I'll see y'all real soon." Heading for the door, I call over my shoulder, "'Night."

The gals all offer friendly farewells, and I traipse out to my Jeep.

Grams is going to be insufferable when she learns her outfit was such a big hit!

THE SHADOWED, EERIE BOOKSTORE sends shivers across my skin as I ease through the door from the alleyway. There's no welcoming committee. Only harsh wind rattling the panes in the historic windows, and an occasional creak from a building that has lounged too long on the same plot of land, fill the silence.

After confirming that the front door is secure, I arm the alarm system and cautiously climb the wrought-iron spiral staircase to the Rare Books Loft.

The quiet, abandoned-feeling tableau among

the aligned oak reading desks shifts dramatically after I tug the candle handle.

The bookcase door barely slides open before an anxious caracal shoots through the gap and growls in my general direction.

"Easy! We're on the same team, remember?"

Pyewacket's large golden eyes glint in the near darkness, and he dives back into the apartment. Once the opening is wide enough for me and my hips, I step through and search the ether for Grams.

"Isadora? Myrtle Isadora, are you here?"

She floats out of the closet like goose down on a summer breeze. A woman who hasn't a care in the world. "Oh, how was your day, sweetie?"

Ripping off my thick layer of outerwear, I allow the huge, puffy coat to drop to the plush carpets as I point two fingers at my ridiculous outfit. "How was my day? Have you lost your mind?"

Her shimmering head lazily rolls in my direction, and upon catching sight of me, she blinks like a circuit board gone crazy. Various parts of her ghostly aura spark and flash in contradiction until, finally, she gathers her wits and whooshes toward me. "Oh, Mitzy! What's happening? I lost all track of time. I think I was in Paris, with Max . . ."

"There will be time enough for tales of your many ex-husbands later. Right now we need to update the murder wall and write some new names on those 3 x 5 cards, missy!"

She snaps to ghostly attention and pops a sarcastic salute. "Yes, sir."

Ignoring her performance, I head into the closet. "First things first. I'm going to get out of this insane wardrobe."

After yanking the ribbon ties from my hair and scrubbing my fingers through my bone-white haystack, I throw on an oversized T-shirt, picturing an octopus with a different delectable pastry in each tentacle. The tagline beneath reads, "Many hands make bite work."

As I emerge from the closet I've nicknamed *Sex and the City* meets *Confessions of a Shopaholic*, Grams dutifully hovers above a stack of 3 x 5 cards, pen in glowing hand. "Ready when you are, Captain."

"Oh, knock it off. I don't actually have that much information." A deep breath for strength, and I push on. "Obviously, we'll have to make cards for all the gals in the wrestling league. But let the record show, I honestly don't suspect a single one."

Grams scribbles away on the cards as I recite the names. "Psychic confirmation of their innocence?"

"Not at all. Just a regular old human gut feeling."

Pyewacket hops onto the bureau and swats angrily at my jewelry box. "What's up, Pye? Did you lose something?"

"Reow." Can confirm.

As a humble servant to Mr. Cuddlekins, I approach the jewelry box and open it immediately. His black-tufted ears twitch, and he carefully extends his claws, attempting to hook one through the engagement ring I tucked away for safe keeping before practice.

"Hold on! That belongs to me. Under no circumstances are you allowed to play with, hide, or in any other way disturb my engagement ring."

Ghost-ma clears her throat in the background. "Technically, it's my ring. In case we've all forgotten, Odell sealed his vows to me with that very ring."

Bowing mockingly, I acknowledge. "Yes, dearest grandmother. We are all quite aware of the ring's provenance." I'm pleased to use the word taught to me by my wizened mentor, Silas Willoughby. "However, much like the rest of your estate, it has passed to me. Not to mention, Erick proposed to *me* with that ring. So it's my engagement ring now."

She crosses her ethereal arms and offers a bit of a huff, but it's impossible for her to hide the brilliant glow of her aura. Nothing has made her happier in the three-plus years I've known her than Erick's magical, romantic proposal.

"Well, what's wrong with that, dear?"

Walking toward her with the threatening glare of an apex predator, I point a single finger to my lips — which did not move — and exhale like an angry grizzly.

"Mitzy, I'm sorry. It gets all jumbled up in here. Please, forgive an old woman her mistakes."

A particularly hilarious comment coming from a ghost whose chronological age exceeds her appearance by at least thirty years. Apparently, when she crossed to the in-between, she was allowed to pick the ghost-age of her choice.

Rolling my eyes, I offer an insincere truce. "Fine."

Back to the furry fiend. As I attempt to close the jewelry box, Pyewacket hits me with a warning swat. I can assure you it's a warning, because he kindly retracts his needle-like claws.

"What's the deal? What did I ever do to you?" Once again, he slaps a large tan paw toward my engagement ring.

"Oh, I think I get it now. Here's the deal, son. I can't wear it when I'm undercover. Don't worry, I'm not out carousing behind Erick's back. I'm on a case. And I would never do anything to jeopardize my relationship with the delicious Sheriff Too-Hot-To-Handle."

With that, I exert my opposable-thumb-based human superiority and close the box. Pyewacket leaps from the bureau and disappears into the closet. Somewhere in that Narnia-like realm, he has a secret escape passage.

I have yet to discover it.

Time to return to the task at hand. Grams brings me the index cards, and I tack them to the rolling corkboard. Using green yarn, I make the connections I've discovered so far. Sadly, everyone on the list is connected to everyone else.

"We have to crack this case, Grams. Tanya was a saint to these women. There's got to be another avenue, or someone in the mix that we're overlooking."

"Well, you mentioned that Dylan Bernard isn't too thrilled about the women's league. He seems like the obvious suspect."

"You're not wrong. Do you think I should tell Erick?"

She places a bejeweled fist on her curvy hip and narrows her gaze. "I think we've all seen what happens when you withhold evidence. It's especially dangerous now that you're engaged. I think you need to share your intel immediately."

As I grab my phone to fire off a text, a sudden

thought bombards me from the ether. "Are you just trying to get Erick to come over?"

Ghost-ma attempts to steal one of my moves by painting her features in the portrait of innocence and avoiding a verbal answer.

Exhaling in defeat, I fire off a text. "I might have a break in the case. You still at work?"

Less than a heartbeat later —

BING. BONG. BING. The bell for the alleyway door resounds through the empty bookstore.

I lock eyes with Ghost-ma. "He's here!"

My phone pings with a text from Erick. "My secret psychic."

Warm tingles flush my skin, and I hardly notice the sharp chill in the air as I hurry downstairs to receive my gentleman caller.

When the door squeaks open, and Erick catches sight of me in nothing more than an oversize T-shirt, his eyes linger on my bare legs.

He hops across the threshold and quickly pulls the door closed behind him. "We better get you upstairs, stat, young lady."

Sheriff Harper scoops me into his arms, and I giggle as I pretend to fight all the way to the apartment. Grams circles overhead, grinning from ear to ear.

"Ahem. I should warn you, Erick, Isadora needs to say her hellos before she says her goodbyes."

He shivers with a ghost chill as Grams swoops near. He can't see or hear my interfering ghost, but the shivers are the only clue he needs — now that he's in the know.

Her designer-gown-clad shoulders slump. "Tell him I said good evening. And that he's the kindest man I've ever met."

"She says hello, and she's heaping you with compliments, as usual."

He chuckles. "As always, thank you, Isadora. Mitzy tells me you're doing a bang-up job planning the wedding. And I appreciate you both keeping my mother in the loop, even though she's living in Florida now."

Erick drops me rather unceremoniously on the overstuffed settee and bends to loosen the ties on his combat boots.

"Grams, have you been writing letters to Gracie Harper?"

"Don't worry. I've been signing your name."

My jaw hangs like half a broken nutcracker. "What? You've been signing my name? Oh brother."

My fiancé plunks down beside me and tenderly rubs my shoulder. "Don't worry. From everything I've heard, the letters couldn't be sweeter."

"That's what I'm afraid of."

Ghost-ma lifts her chin and tsks.

"All right, Grams. You've had your fun. Now, toodle-oo."

She vanishes with a pop and a hiss.

Drama queen.

"She's finally taken her leave."

Before I can add any additional snark, Erick scoops me into an embrace and kisses the sass right off my lips.

Whooooo! I could get used to this.

CHAPTER 8

THE EVENTS OF LAST NIGHT escalated rapidly, and I neglected to deploy the blackout shades used to cover the large bank of 6 x 6 windows facing the great lake behind my bookshop. So, instead of sleeping through Sheriff Harper's early morning exit, I'm wide awake and desperate for coffee.

Not bothering to stifle an overzealous yawn, I ask, "Hey, do you have time for breakfast at the diner?"

Erick turns, his uniform shirt hanging open, and I inhale sharply as I gaze at his marvelous abs.

Jokingly, he points two fingers toward his face. "Hey, I'm up here, Moon."

Giggling uncontrollably, I hightail it to the bathroom, splash some cold water on my face, and tame my tousled hair.

He calls from the main room. "I can probably do a quick breakfast. And I think we both know you're not one to linger over food. So, how fast can you be ready?"

Tempting fate, I shout, "Three minutes."

As I emerge from the bathroom, his thumb hits the timer on his phone, and he pantomimes firing a starting pistol into the air. "Go!"

Flying into the closet, I rip off my oversize T-shirt, grab a familiar pair of skinny jeans, and any sweater I can get my hands on. Just when I think I'm ahead of the curve, I'm helpless to find socks. Rifling through several of the built-in drawers, I finally uncover a thick woolen pair that will have to do.

Running out of the closet, I announce, "Ready!"

He glances at the phone and shakes his head. "Boots and coat, Moon. Ready doesn't mean half ready."

I throw myself onto the overstuffed settee, shove my feet into the boots, and retrieve my giant coat from the floor. As I'm about to slip my left arm in and claim the win, Erick shouts, "That's time. Sorry. You lose. I believe you said loser buys breakfast?"

Hanging my head in mock shame, I grumble out my reply. "As per usual."

Erick pulls me close, and we walk in brisk

unison as though we're taking part in a three-legged race. We burst into the warmth of the diner with rosy cheeks and healthy appetites.

Odell gives us the standard spatula salute and we grab a booth. Steaming mugs of coffee join us a moment later, and Tally nods pleasantly as she makes her way toward the four-top by the front window.

"Hey, I have some news on the case."

"Classic left field from Moon." Erick leans back against the red-vinyl bench seat and crosses his arms in that yummy way that makes his biceps bulge. "Are you holding out on me?"

"Hardly! You didn't give me a chance to put two words together when you showed up last night. You were a man on a mission. And that mission was not solving this case."

He blushes adorably and leans forward. "What have you got for me?"

"Did you know Dylan Bernard had it in for the women's wrestling league? Sounds like Tanya went up against him in several legal battles to protect the sport. I mean, that's what I heard."

At first, he nods absently, but then a strange spark ignites his gaze. "Mitzy? What aren't you telling me?"

"Me? I'm telling you everything. This Dylan

Bernard guy is totally a bad seed. He definitely could be the suspect you're looking for."

Erick rubs his left thumb along his stubbled jaw and narrows his gaze. "Mmhmm. And when did you become such an expert on the women's wrestling league?"

Oops. Busted.

I toy with the idea of giving Pilar all the credit, but we've repeatedly promised to be completely honest with each other. Maybe there's a way I can share the information without —

He waves his hand in front of my face. "Hey, I know that look. Don't waste your time coming up with a story to cover your story."

Blerg. "All right. I'll give it to you straight, but you have to promise not to yell at me."

He quickly reaches a hand across the table and squeezes one of mine tenderly. "I would never yell at you. Yes, I get worried when you put yourself at unnecessary risk, but I would never raise my voice to you, Mitzy. That's a promise."

The warmth of trust floods my heart, and I spill my guts.

"So you're a lady wrestler now?"

My extrasensory perception picks up on an interesting combination of concern and intrigue.

Throwing on my Cherry Darling accent, I give him a little taste. "Yes, sir. Cherry Darling should be on the card this Saturday and hopes to be the new hero of the league. Thank you kindly."

Odell arrives with our plates near the end of my speech, and the two men share an unnecessarily long chuckle at my expense.

Erick sizes up his blueberry pancakes while I cross my arms and glare at both of them. "It's not funny. I'm undercover, and I'm getting some great information. First and foremost, none of those women are responsible for what happened. They all loved Tanya. They would have done anything for her. Those ladies take their wrestling seriously, and Tanya was like a savior to them."

Odell shakes his head, raps his knuckles twice on the silver-flecked white Formica table, and returns to the kitchen without comment.

Erick takes another bite of his pancakes, washes it down with some java, and smiles. "On the matter of the wrestlers, you and I are in agreement. I can't imagine any of them hurting Tanya. However, every one of those women has other people in her life. And I think you'll find, if you dig a little deeper, several of them have unsavory pasts."

I'm halfway through my breakfast and my cup of go-go juice. My regular senses are beginning to catch up with my extra ones. "So, you're saying I should stay undercover and continue to gather intel?"

He opens his mouth to protest, but I hold up a finger and continue. "Remember, I signed that confidential informant agreement with the Birch County Sheriff's Department, and I'm an honorary deputy. I think you'll find I can be quite useful, Sheriff Harper."

He shakes his head, exhales, and finishes his breakfast without comment. I'll take his silence as agreement.

Jumping up, I bus our dishes while he slips on his thick brown uniform jacket.

Erick kisses me sweetly on the cheek and exits the diner.

I pop into the kitchen to chew the fat with my grandpa. "What do you know about the women's wrestling league?"

"Not much. Wrestling was never my sport. But I sat on the board of the women's shelter for a couple years. That Tanya was a real firecracker. She went far above and beyond to make sure those women were safe and protected. She even saw to the complete relocation of the safe house after that incident last year."

I'd never heard a whisper of the incident, but my psychic senses are buzzing for more information. "What incident was that?"

Odell runs a hand through his high-and-tight grey buzz cut and shakes his head. "The old brain bucket ain't what it used to be. Things get more jumbled up in there with each passing year. I'm sure there's a report at the station. Too bad you don't know someone there to help you out." His coarse chuckle is as comforting to me as a cozy flannel shirt.

"I'll head over there and see what I can find. If you're right, maybe that will point the investigation in the right direction. Thanks, Gramps."

He nods, and deep lines crinkle around his dark eyes as he smiles.

Time to search through a bunch of boring old reports to see if I can find a hot new lead.

CHAPTER 9

When I waltz into the sheriff's station, Deputy Baird, a.k.a. Furious Monkeys, does not look up from her phone. This is hardly a recent development. She plays at the tippy-top level in this game and takes it quite seriously. We've developed a series of head nods that replace any need for actual speech or eye contact. She tilts her head toward the crooked swinging gate, and I proceed with ease.

If I thought my sashay through the bullpen would be as simple as my entrance, I couldn't have been more sadly mistaken.

"Back here to poke around in our case, Moon?" Deputy Paulsen immediately gets to her feet and strides around her metal desk to intercept me. Her hand rests comfortably on her holstered gun, and her expression is as unwelcoming as usual.

This woman knows exactly how to push my buttons. "Glad to see you chose to stay on board after the election."

There's a flash of hurt in her eyes, and I instantly regret taking things too far. "Sorry, Pauly. I shouldn't have said that."

Her guard rockets up, and she snarls like the schoolyard bully she usually is. "Sheriff's in his office." Pauly Paulsen pushes past me and heads toward the break room, but not before my psychic senses take a punch in the gut.

That was definitely hitting below the belt, and I, of all people, should know better.

When I round the corner into Sheriff Harper's office, Erick's weak smile tells me everything I need to know about the current case. "Hey, Moon, I hope you have some good news."

"Maybe. Are you bringing in Dylan Bernard?"

"Done."

"What? Why didn't you tell me? I'm sure I could've —"

Erick shakes his head and groans. "Nothing to tell. He came in, and the second I mentioned Tanya's name, he called his lawyer. His attorney was here in a flash and advised him not to comment on any ongoing legal actions. Total and complete dead end."

"Did you sense anything, though?" I step forward hopefully.

"I don't have your skills, Moon. I have to work the evidence, and right now, that's pretty thin." He hangs his head and it nearly breaks my heart.

Taking a seat in one of the uncomfortable scarred wooden chairs, I slouch forward. "I might have something. I was hoping you'd give me a peek at an old police report."

He exhales and shrugs. "I guess. What's it regarding?"

"There was a kerfuffle at the previous women's shelter last year. I understand it forced them to relocate the facility. Is there an incident report I can look at?"

He nods and gets to his feet. "Be right back."

Entertaining myself by counting the dents in his well-used metal file cabinet, time moves slower than molasses in January. After what seems like hours —

"This is probably what you're looking for. Do you think it has something to do with Tanya's murder?"

"Only one way to find out." I take the report, shift my abilities to high, and scan the pages. A man named Cobb Astley broke into the shelter and attempted to kidnap a woman named Raelyn Engle. However, in the witness statements,

Raelyn insists that Cobb wasn't trying to harm her. They had recently started dating, and he was attempting to save her from her abusive ex-husband.

Sounds sketchy.

How he obtained the location of the safe house was even more unsettling. He stated he had followed Raelyn to the shelter to make sure she got there safely, and returned the next evening to save her — yet again.

According to the report, the police did not question the ex-husband, and there's no mention of why Cobb thought she was in imminent danger.

The overall vibe is confusing. My extrasensory antennae pick up several partial truths, but no smoking gun.

When I lift my eyes from the page, I'm met by the sultry grin of my handsome fiancé. My tummy flip-flops, and my cheeks blush. "What are you looking at, Sheriff?"

His grin widens. "I'm looking at the best thing that ever happened to me."

Initially, I'm flattered, but then my self-sabotage brain remembers an earlier conversation. "So all that stuff you said at the crime scene . . . You didn't mean it?"

"There are two sides to every coin, right?" He sighs wistfully and continues to smile at me with love and admiration. The *feels* are rolling across the desk.

"Copy that. Can I pump you for some more info?"

He exhales and chuckles helplessly. "I honestly don't think I can say no to you."

Smiling brazenly, I lean forward and run my finger across the back of his hand. "Let's hope those powers never fade."

Loud throat clearing in the doorway interrupts our intimate moment. "Got a couple of the wrestlers here for questioning. You want me to put them in room two or separate 'em?" Deputy Paulsen looks disgusted by our semi-private display of affection.

Glancing at Erick in sheer panic, I search the small office for a hiding place. Fortunately, he doesn't need psychic powers to read my mind.

"Tell the ladies to hang tight in the lobby. I need to get some papers together before I call them back to interrogation."

"10-4."

Paulsen leaves without protest, and Erick jumps up to close the door. "I'll set one up in each interrogation room. That should give you time to get into observation. I think there were only two coming in today, but I'll make sure the coast is clear. I know it goes against your core being, but do you think you can sit patiently in the observation room and wait for the 'all clear'?"

"Rude. I'll try my best."

He rolls his eyes, exits the office, and pulls the door closed tightly behind him.

Oh brother. Sheriff Harper is an even worse actor than me. His voice is unnaturally loud as he escorts the women down the hallway and gives instructions.

"You go ahead and have a seat in room one, and you head into room two. I'll take the statement in one first."

There's some shuffling in the hallway, and first, one door closes firmly then the next. I wait a beat, crack the door open to double-check, and race into the observation room.

Rita Riot is in room one. I flip the silver toggle and listen carefully.

Erick gets her details, and it takes me a moment to process the fact that she has a *real* name. It seems obvious, but it never occurred to me at practice.

"What was your relationship with Ms. Tucker?"

Rita smiles warmly. "Pretty simple. I was spiraling into a super dark place. I got out of the women's penitentiary, and no one would hire me. I was about a heartbeat from returning to —" She stares at the sheriff like a caged animal.

"I don't plan on bringing any charges for things that happened in the past. Please continue." Erick's voice offers the reassurance she needs.

"I was in touch with some people from my past, and I was considering some less than legal work."

He nods.

"Tanya walked into this diner in Broken Rock where I was literally spending my last couple of bucks on coffee and a day-old bagel. She took one look at me, sat down in the chair opposite, and simply said, 'I can help.'"

Sheriff Harper offers a smile.

"I swear to you, Sheriff, there was a halo floating over her head that day, and for me, it never disappeared."

Wiping a traitorous tear from my cheek, I double down on my commitment to finding the person who took this amazing woman from us.

Erick nods. "Thank you. Were you aware of anyone who would want to harm Ms. Tucker?"

Rita grimaces. I can sense the reality of so violently losing Tanya hitting Rita again. She hangs her head. "I hate to tell you how long that list was, Sheriff. For every person she helped, there was another person she pissed off. If you'll pardon my French." Rita looks directly at Erick. "I can tell you my old gang wasn't too happy to hear they'd lost their safecracker."

Sheriff Harper slides a paper and pen across the table. "If you could provide me with a list of names, it would really help us out."

Rita leans away from the paper as though he's placed a scorpion on the table.

Erick pushes his advantage. "Forensics has almost nothing to go on. If we can't get any useful information from people who knew her best, this murderer might walk free."

From my side of the one-way glass, I can feel Rita struggling. She doesn't want to be a snitch, but her admiration for Tanya wins out in the end.

She nods and takes the pen.

Sheriff Harper thanks her, gets to his feet, and heads over to room two.

Sitting across the table from him is Ivana Vodka, out of her stereotypical Russian wardrobe and wearing a faded army jacket.

Once the sheriff gets her particulars, he attempts to build some rapport. "Where did you serve?"

Her eyes widen with surprise, and Erick gently gestures toward her coat. Ivana's shoulders drop, and she nods. "I was in Afghanistan. But I'm ashamed to say I rocked out."

He leans forward, and his voice carries no judgment. "AWOL or drugs?"

Again, her eyes round with shock.

Erick leans forward. "I served two tours. I've seen it all."

She breathes a heavy sigh. "Drugs. It was incredibly easy to get your hands on heroin over there. I thought I could control it, you know."

He nods. "I've seen firsthand how it destroys good soldiers. What happened when you got home?"

She stiffens, and her gaze immediately falls to the floor. "I went hard in the paint, Sheriff. I'm ashamed to say I lost everything before I tried to get right. When Tanya turned up at that methadone clinic and offered me a job picking up laundry from shut-ins . . ."

Erick can clearly see a theme developing. "How long have you been clean?"

"Two years, three months, one week, three days —" she looks at her phone "— and fifteen hours."

He straightens in his chair. "Keep it up. Is there anyone you know of who wanted to hurt Ms. Tucker?"

It doesn't escape my notice that he left out the question about what Ivana was doing on the day in question. Clearly, he believes her to be innocent.

She attempts a chuckle. "I suppose my dealer wasn't too happy."

Erick offers her a piece of paper, a pen, and a

judgment-free zone to make a list.

Ivana doesn't hesitate for a moment. She picks up the pen and nods once. "Anything I can do to help, Sheriff."

He steps out of room two and returns to escort Rita from the station. A few minutes later, he takes Ivana out as well.

It feels like the coast is clear, but someone specifically warned me to wait patiently.

To be clear, I'm waiting, but it's anything but patient.

The door opens, and Erick drops into a chair beside me. "Well, those two women didn't have anything to do with Tanya's death."

Wiping an errant tear from my cheek, I nod my agreement. "Yeah, I had no idea how much Tanya was secretly doing for this community."

"You better get out of here while you can, Moon. I have more women to question from the league, and we don't want to blow your cover. I'll look into Rita's gang connections and see if there are any good leads on the other woman's list, but I feel like I'm barely treading water."

"Were you serious? You told Rita there was no forensic evidence?"

He shakes his head. "Nah, just an old cop trick. Gotta make 'em feel like they're my only hope if I want to get any useful information."

"Oh, that's a good one. Do you have a report from the medical examiner?"

"Preliminary. The ME was an acquaintance of Tanya's and put this case at the top of her list. Unfortunately, the killer must've worn gloves because there was no DNA evidence in the wound, only some fibers from the rope on her skin."

"Rope? Tanya was strangled with a rope?"

"Oh, sorry. I thought you'd already sensed that, or whatever."

Shaking my head in horror, I attempt to steady my swirling gut. "Not the details. What about under her fingernails? She seemed to really put up a fight."

"Still waiting on the results. There's a chance she scratched her attacker, but we won't be sure till tomorrow. I'll text you when I find out for sure."

Silence hangs in the air, and Erick leans forward expectantly. "Normally, you're a little more excited about getting information on a case. What's up?"

"Um, I'm gonna be kind of busy tomorrow."

He scrunches up his face. "Too busy for a text?"

After a long exhale, I attempt to screw my courage to the sticking place. "Yeah, I'm on the card."

I expect Erick to chuckle. I do not expect a full-blown guffaw.

CHAPTER 10

I'm not sure why I ever bother to set an alarm. My bossy caracal always manages to roust me before the poor little alarm on my phone has a prayer.

This morning he simply rolls over from the two-thirds of the bed he's been occupying and climbs onto my chest.

The difficulty of drawing breath into my lungs rips me from dreamland.

Real shame, too. Erick and I were horseback riding along the white sands of some exotic beach. I can still feel the sun on my shoulders and the salty air swirling around us as we raced along the shore with wild abandon.

"RE-ow." Feed me.

Grabbing my phone, I groan loudly and turn off the alarm that would have awakened me ten minutes from now. "You need to get your internal clock checked, son. It's incredibly rude to wake up your human companion before her official alarm."

Pyewacket squeezes his eyelids closed in extreme disinterest.

I wiggle out from beneath his heft and make a beeline for my bathrobe. This old building is draftier than I'd like. Thankfully, I've upped the insulation factor on the remodel and added in-floor heating in the primary bedroom and the open-plan main floor.

No sooner have I tied my robe snugly around me than Mr. Cuddlekins utters a warning.

"Ree-OW!" A warning punctuated by a threat.

"Wow, you are low-key irritating this morning, Pye. I'm moving as fast as I can. As you well know, I wouldn't dare leave the premises without seeing to your precious food bowl."

He turns his head and attempts to thwack the twisted ivy medallion as he stretches up on his hind legs.

"Take it easy. I'm coming." Pressing the button that opens the secret door, I trudge downstairs to do my master's bidding. However, when I set the heaping bowl of sugary children's cereal on the floor, my furry overlord is nowhere to be found.

"Robin Pyewacket Goodfellow! You woke me up ten minutes early in some sort of food panic, and now you've disappeared? What in all of *Moonrise Kingdom* are you up to?"

A thundering crash in the bookstore causes momentary heart palpitations. As I rush toward the noise, it becomes clear that it was no accident. Pyewacket crouches atop the stacks, and it seems his powerful foreleg was used to displace not one but three books.

Having learned my lesson the hard way, I obediently stoop and retrieve the titles. Rather than angrily re-shelving them, I accept them for what they are — clues.

"Let's see what you've curated for us today. Book 1: *Mastering Your Marriage*; Book 2: *Avoiding Relationship Ruts*; Book 3: *Is He Mr. Right or Mr. Run?*"

Now that I've scanned the books and have mental images to refer to using my psychic replay skills, I re-shelve them and scowl at the mischievous caracal.

"What on earth are you getting at, Pye? Erick and I have a great relationship. We've gotten all our secrets out on the table, and we discuss everything. I mean, we seem to be having a little debate about my sleuthing, but it's nothing serious. Nothing I need self-help books to solve."

"Ree-ow." Soft but condescending.

I'm not sure I like this cat's attitude. "Breakfast awaits you in the back room, m'lord."

With that, I stomp upstairs and begin preparing for the wrestling match.

Grams insists on heavy eyeliner, tons of hairspray, and bobby pins. She even wants me to put foundation on the part of my stomach that will be peeking out between my knotted cherry-print top and my ridiculous shorts.

A bridge too far. "I will do no such thing, Isadora. This is an undercover operation, not a career change. I look the part enough to get the information I need."

"It never hurts to go the extra mile, dear. And I hope you win your game today."

"I'm sure you meant match. You know more about wrestling than me."

"Yes, of course. Match." With no further poking or prodding, she floats silently to the desk in the corner.

I don't exactly have time for a sit-down breakfast at the diner. Plus, I'd rather avoid the prying eyes of townspeople or the unavoidable questions from my grandfather. Instead, I'll grab coffee and a couple chocolate croissants from the patisserie.

I'm an old hand at eating and driving. Croissants are a little flakier than the cheap gas-station doughnuts I used to buy back in Arizona, but all in all, I manage to wolf down my sugar-based breakfast before I pull into the fairgrounds.

The place has a whole new look today. The parking lot has been freshly plowed, and someone either shoveled or used a snowblower to create a wide path to the exhibition hall.

There's an enormous sign stapled to the wooden building, listing all the matches taking place today. At the bottom of the list, in huge letters, is the title match between Anna Mel Cracker and Ivana Vodka.

My match is third from the top. I'm wrestling Hallucna Jenn, and I have no idea what our beef is supposed to be.

Better find Anna Mel and get the details along with some last-minute pointers.

Inside, a crew of super fans is setting up folding chairs, the announcer's table, and several remote speakers.

The familiar faces of my cohorts turn, and some even smile. However, Anna Mel is not among them.

I find Rita Riot and see what she knows. Time for some Southern charm. "Hey, I had a few questions for Anna Mel. Any idea where she's hidin'?"

Rita scans the room and shrugs. "I saw her truck pull into the lot right behind me. I thought she came in. Beats me. Maybe she forgot something in her vehicle."

For some reason, that particular sentence causes the mood ring on my left hand to burn with fiery insistence.

Glancing down, I see a powerful hand gripping someone's neck.

No time to waste. "Thanks. I'll find her."

Glad to have my jacket around me, I burst out of the exhibition hall and desperately scan the parking lot.

Sadly, there are several trucks in the parking lot.

I need to stop panicking and use my extra abilities.

Taking a deep breath, I calm my emotions and reach out for any sign of Anna Mel.

The word "dumpster" slams into my ear as though fired from a slingshot.

Racing toward the side of the building, I hear angry voices. Screeching to a halt just before the corner, I lean against the building and listen with every part of my being.

"This wasn't supposed to happen!"

I recognize that voice as Anna Mel.

"Don't tell me what was supposed to happen, Lynn. You think I don't know what was supposed to happen? Are you calling me stupid?"

Risking a peek around the corner, I gasp when I see a large male figure manhandling the formidable Anna Mel Cracker.

Not on my watch.

Rushing toward the pair, I blast my foot into the back of one of his knees, and he falls to the ground, shouting angrily.

I grab Anna Mel's hand and tug her toward the building. "Come on. I'll call the cops."

She twists her hand around my forearm and yanks me to a halt. "Mind your own business, Cherry."

My throat goes dry, and a moment later, a psychic flash fills in the information I wish I'd had sixty seconds ago.

Anna Mel Cracker, a.k.a. Lynn, a.k.a. Raelyn Engle. That can only mean one thing about the man on the ground. He's gotta be the guy from the "incident" last year.

"Cobb Astley, I reckon you best stay down. I don't know what Lynn's trouble is, but I ain't got no problem callin' the 5-0."

The broad-shouldered guy on the ground turns an angry face in my direction as he rubs his wounded knee. A thick beard and heavy mustache cover most of his face, and a stocking cap pulled snugly over his hair takes care of the rest. All I can see are two beady, furious, dark eyes. However, he seems to take my threat seriously.

"I got no idea what's put a burr under your saddle, and, frankly, I don't care. We have a big day, and the team needs our coach."

Gesturing for Anna Mel to lead the way into the building, I press my lips together defiantly. "Lead the way, coach. We only have thirty minutes till the first match, and I know the ladies would love a pep talk."

Her expression is angry, but fortunately, I have other senses to rely on. The energy beneath the hard exterior is one of fear mixed with relief.

To his credit, the big man stays down until we reach the corner of the building. Just outside the door, she grips my arm and spins me toward her with a force she had no intention of using on Cobb Astley. "Look, Cherry, you didn't see anything, okay?"

Twisting my arm from her grasp, I lift both hands in the air in a gesture of surrender and lean into my southern accent. "Hey, I ain't interested in y'alls' issues. I'm just lookin' out for the team. We all want what's best for the league, right?"

Her features soften, and she nods.

We march into the building, and she instantly embodies her wrestling identity. She is calm, collected, and in charge.

A curtained area in the far corner is reserved for our team. Anna Mel gathers us and walks everyone through the matches on the card. Apparently, no one needs a reason to fight Hallucna Jenn. She just shows up and kicks the butt of whoever happens to be in her line of sight. Since I'm the fresh meat on the team, Anna Mel and Rita thought that would be a compelling catalyst for the match.

I'm paraphrasing.

Speakers crackle to life, and the announcer's voice bounces off the high ceiling. "Birch County wrestling fans! Get ready to roar!"

No turning back now . . .

CHAPTER 11

STAGE FRIGHT CONSUMES ME. The first two matches seem to be over in the blink of an eye. Before I can make plans to run away, I hear my name over the speakers.

"Joining us today from the Lone Star State, Cherrrrrry Daaaaaarling!"

Someone shoves me through the haphazardly hung curtains, and I swallow hard as I attempt to embody the *darling* of the South.

Adding some extra wiggle to my waddle, I wave and blow kisses to the audience as I approach the ring. There was no sign of Hallucna Jenn backstage. I'm sure she's planning to make an unforgettable entrance.

For once, my roll under the ropes looks semiprofessional, and I hop to my feet inside the squared circle.

As I strut around the ring and continue to blow kisses, the hoots and hollers increase. Maybe I really can be a hero . . .

With no warning, an insane shriek echoes from the rafters as a Hallucna Jenn swings down in a clearly not-up-to-code harness.

If not for my psychic senses, she would've connected with the back of my head and probably knocked me out in the first round!

She snaps out of her quick-release harness and turns on me like a wild beast.

I haven't learned much about wrestling lore, but I've learned that delayed gratification builds suspense. As she shoves me toward the turnbuckle, I take the hit and go down with a splash of southern charm.

The feral wrestler leaps on top of me, and the referee hits the mat to start the count out.

Just before we hit that critical number three, I launch Hallucna Jenn off of me and crawl to the ropes.

Cheers burst from the crowd, and several spectators get to their feet.

Hey, I'm getting the hang of this.

Pulling myself up, one rope at a time, I struggle to catch my breath.

Hallucna Jenn comes at me with the fury of a crazed creature. She grips me and, despite her stature, somehow flips me upside down to put me in position for her signature pile-driver move.

Newsflash: Cherry Darling is not going out in a blaze of head-smashing glory.

As she lifts me in preparation to drive my skull into the mat, I hook my legs around her neck and pull her over the top of me, like a two-person somersault. Shockingly, it works!

I'm not even sure what happened. I feel like I channeled Ronda Rousey for a hot minute!

Before Hallucna Jenn can fully recover, I flip her over, yank her from the mat by her hair, and circle my arm around her neck.

A couple of the wrestler *plants* in the audience clap and yell, "Put her to sleep, Cherry!" and, "Choke her! Choke her out!"

I better give the crowd what they want. Flashing a sassy grin/wink combo, I hook the left arm over the right wrist and slowly apply pressure.

Hallucna Jenn kicks and scratches like a captured werewolf, but my hold is locked in.

Leaning back and mugging for the audience, I feel her go limp in my arms.

I release my opponent from the hold, and she drops to the mat with a thud of finality. I climb as high as the bottom rope at the turnbuckle and lift my arms into the air in celebration.

Whistles, whoops, and hollers echo through the exhibition hall.

However, when I catch sight of a particular spectator, all the cherry-red in my foolish blouse rushes to my cheeks.

Who invited the sheriff?

Leaping from the turnbuckle, I run to the center of the ring, where Hallucna Jenn is starting to regain consciousness. The referee lifts my arm in the air, and the bell rings. I'm officially the winner.

There's a tingle from the mood ring on my left hand, but there's no time to sneak a peek. I have to take my bows and avoid Erick. If any of these gals see me making nice with the sheriff, it won't end well for my investigation.

I head back behind the curtain to see if anyone needs help with their wardrobe.

A couple minutes later, Hallucna Jenn staggers in and puts her hand on my shoulder. "Mad props, Cherry. I've never seen anyone get out of my pile-driver before. You gotta teach me that move. The crowd went wild! Glad to have you aboard."

Unsure how to react in such an oddly supportive environment, I do as my mama taught me and nod and smile.

Peeking through the curtains, I see no sign of

Sheriff Harper. Granted, he was in civilian clothes, so he wouldn't have drawn too much attention. Another bit of good news is that there's no sign of Cobb Astley.

Finally, the title match between Ivana Vodka and Anna Mel Cracker arrives. They wrestle with amazing vigor for almost twenty minutes!

The tide shifts back and forth, and even I have no idea who will come out the victor.

At the last minute, something unbelievable happens! Candy Cornwell and Anita Gurney approach the ring from opposite sides. One rolls under the bottom rope and the other leaps over the top. The match suddenly turns into a quartet, and it's hard to keep track of who's going after whom.

Anita bounces Ivana off the ropes, sending her sprawling on the mat. Candy climbs to the top rope to perform her signature move — leaping from the top of the turnbuckle to literally crush her opponent. As she crouches to spring from the turnbuckle, the entire post cracks away from the main structure, sending Candy crashing unceremoniously into the dangerously unpadded corner of the ring.

My mood rings burns with an urgent message.

A hush falls over the crowd.

Glancing down, I see a quick flash of a wrench

loosening the turnbuckle bolts. Candy's crash was no accident. Is it connected to Tanya's murder?

"Ladies and gentlemen, please stay in your seats. There's been a serious malfunction with our safety equipment. Can someone grab the paramedics?"

A moment later, the door bursts open, and two paramedics bustle in with the gurney in tow.

Anna Mel helps them transfer Candy to the backboard, and they wheel her out of the exhibition hall, which stands in near silence.

The announcer attempts to reassure the crowd. "We all wish Candy Cornwell a swift recovery. You'll have to come back next month if you want to see how this match is going to end. Looks like Ivana Vodka will be marching out of Red Square to take her revenge. Thank you all for coming today, and remember, our women's wrestling league is nothing without its fans! The ladies will be signing autographs for the next fifteen minutes, so get in line fast if you want a souvenir."

Signing autographs? Oh brother.

Rita Riot slips an arm around me and shoves me toward the makeshift reception line forming in front of what was, only moments ago, the announcer's table.

Scores of fans line up and offer their single-sheet, photocopied programs for signing. I may have come up with a good name for my secret identity, but I hadn't really practiced a signature! Luckily, I'm a quick study.

After signing autographs for well beyond fifteen minutes, Anna Mel cracks her whip and the wrestlers march back to the curtained area.

The volunteers clear out the exhibition hall, and Anna Mel asks us all to take a knee for Candy. After an appropriate moment of silence. Each of the ladies grabs their cold-weather gear and heads to their cars. Hanging back, I hope to get a final word with Anna Mel before she leaves.

Fortunately, luck is on my side.

Staying in character, I throw on my accent. "Hey, Anna, can I ask ya somethin'?"

She turns. "You did great today. If you're looking for any feedback, you don't need it. You're a natural out there."

"It's not about the match. It's about what happened in the parking lot. If y'all are in trouble, I'd do anything in my power to help you."

Any adrenaline left in her system vanishes. The color drains from her face and she looks away. "I've got things under control. It's all good."

My time in the league is running out, and Erick's investigation seems stalled. I'm going to have to push to make progress. "Raelyn, I know sometimes people have trouble breaking patterns in their life. I don't know your whole story, but Cobb seems like he comes with a huge set of problems. Are you sure you couldn't use a wingwoman?"

She peeks through the curtains and nervously scans the empty exhibition hall. "Like I said, it's all good. Nobody knows about all the stuff that went down before I joined the league. Can I trust you to keep quiet about today?"

"Yeah, as long as I know you're safe." Hopefully, the subtle undertone of my reply indicates that if Cobb isn't "safe," I'll no longer keep my trap shut.

Somehow my words seem to give her a moment of comfort, and her shoulders relax. "See you at practice on Monday."

"Yeah. You bet."

She exits the backstage area, and I change from my wrestling boots into my winter boots and secure my warm coat around me.

In the near-empty parking lot, there's no sign of the sheriff's cruiser or my boyfriend's personal vehicle, the bad-boy Nova, so I slip into my Jeep and drive home more confused and stumped than ever.

CHAPTER 12

The depth of my distraction becomes obvious when I turn into the alleyway and have to slam on the brakes to avoid hitting the 1968 copper-brown Chevy Nova SS parked beside the bookshop's alley entrance.

Erick grins through his windshield and backs all the way down the alley, giving me room to pull into the middle garage, where I park the Jeep.

My eager fiancé meets me outside and offers to carry my wrestling boots.

"Are you turning into some kind of women's wrestling ring rat?"

His eyes widen. "Ring rat?"

"Yeah, that's what they call the stalker-y superfans."

He grins and flashes his eyebrows. "I was

hoping I already had superfan status. I was bucking for behind-the-scenes access — no stalking necessary."

Rolling my eyes, I open the alleyway door, and we walk smack dab into my grandmother's ghost.

Spasms of shivers ripple over my boyfriend and he inhales sharply.

I take a different approach. "Grams! There's no need for you to camp out by the door. You're the first person, I mean, ghost, I look for every time I get home."

"Sorry, sweetie. I was all fired up to hear about your match."

"I'll give you all the details after I get changed." As I climb over the "No Admittance" chain at the bottom of the circular staircase, Erick Harper seems to have other ideas.

"Isadora, I feel like you're here. And if you want to hear about Cherry Darling's match, I'm your man." He looks on uneasily as his right arm seems to lift and fall of its own accord and another shiver grips him.

I shout from the top of the staircase, "That's her version of, 'Yes, please.'"

Grams giggles. "Oh, Mitzy. You're such a hoot."

As Erick begins to spin the yarn, I disappear into the apartment to wiggle out of my teeny tiny shorts.

By the time I'm in comfortable yoga pants and a thick sweater, Erick is nearing the end of his tale.

"And then she hooked her legs around the wild girl's head and completely flipped her over 180 degrees!" He's gesturing wildly with his arms, and Grams is enthralled.

"Then she spun around and put her in the sleeper hold! The crowd went nuts."

Isadora zooms toward me. "Sweetie! I got so excited about the wrestling, I nearly forgot about the investigation."

Placing a hand on Erick's arm, I attempt to bring his show to an end. "That'll do, Sheriff. That'll do. What we really need to be talking about is this 'going nowhere' case. Although, I might just have a juicy update."

"Seriously?" Erick looks hopeful for the first time in days.

"Yeah, come on up to the apartment. I'll order some pizza for delivery."

Upstairs, Pyewacket joins our impromptu celebration. He chooses Erick's side of the room and offers his broad tan head for proper scratching.

Sheriff Harper gives the caracal his undivided attention. "Hey, buddy, did you miss me?"

"Reow." Can confirm.

"Watch yourself, Pye. I'm still the keeper of the Fruity Puffs."

Pyewacket gazes in my direction and immediately squeezes his eyelids closed.

Even this four-legged fiend knows the emptiness of my threats.

"What's this new info, Moon?" Erick continues to lavish attention on Pyewacket.

"Before the match got started, there was an incident in the parking lot. I was eavesdropping, so to speak. Part of what I uncovered was regular, and part was extrasensory."

"What happened?" Erick leans forward.

Grams grabs the pen, and when Erick sees it hovering above the stack of 3 x 5 cards, he swallows loudly. "That's going to take a little more getting used to."

Fortunately, he can't hear my grandmother's reply. "Oh, you'll have plenty of time to get used to it when you move in! That renovation is nearly complete."

"Grams is eager for the update as well." Sometimes my job as an afterlife interpreter involves curating what I translate.

"Careful, young lady. I could just as easily write my message out on this card." She places a bejeweled fist on her curvy hip.

Tapping my fingertips together like a cartoon villain, I slap back. "You wouldn't dare. I would take violent and immediate action against your couture."

Ghost-ma gasps and drops the pen.

Erick chuckles. "Are you two having a little tiff?"

"Not anymore. Let's get back to my update. I discovered that Anna Mel Cracker is actually Raelyn Engle. And Cobb Astley is not only still in the picture, but he had his hands around her throat when I interrupted them."

Sheriff Harper immediately stops petting the caracal and prepares to launch into action. "Was he trying to strangle her?"

"I thought the same thing. In the end, it seemed more like he was intimidating her into keeping quiet about something. Unfortunately, I interrupted before I heard enough to find out what she was supposed to keep quiet about."

Erick slides his left thumb along his jaw. "I might have to bring them both in for questioning. I won't reveal what you told me, but somehow I'll get her to give me his name during the course of questioning her. I can make it seem relevant to the investigation of Tanya's murder."

"Sounds good. There's definitely something sketchy about that guy." As I rub a wrestling ache on my leg, a second update flashes to mind. "Oh! There was an accident during the title match."

He shrugs. "There are always staged accidents during the matches."

"This one was different. Candy Cornwell was seriously injured, and I'm pretty sure someone tampered with the bolts on the turnbuckle."

"It might be connected . . . We'll keep it in mind." He leans back and laces his fingers together behind his head. "I have some additional information from the ME as well. They tested those fibers found in the wounds around Tanya's neck. The rope the killer used was made from manila fiber."

"Isn't manila a kind of envelope?" I'm no expert, but this seems pretty basic.

Erick sighs and shakes his head. "In this case, it's not. It's a specific type of rope fiber that comes from the abaca plant. It's most commonly used to make rope fenders."

I'm gripped by a fit of giggles. "Rope fenders? Are you messing with me?"

"Absolutely not. It's a legitimate item. I'm sure you've seen them when you've been down to the marina. They're kind of an oblong structure hanging over the side of the boat made from a specific series of knot patterns. They make the whole piece from rope, and the fender, or bumper, keeps the boat from smashing into another boat or the docks."

"Oh. Got it. Why is that important?"

He tilts his head. "Wow. I'm surprised you haven't already figured it out."

No sooner has he made his smart-alecky remark than my psychic senses bail me out. "Whoever strangled Tanya might work on the docks." I quickly clap for myself.

"Possibly." He shrugs. "It's not the only thing that manila fiber is used for, but it's the most common use in this area. It's the first lead we've really had, so I had Deputy Johnson follow up. When you mentioned Cobb Astley, I was only half-surprised. I'm pretty sure I saw that name on the list of employees working at the marina. That could give us probable cause."

"Let me know when they're coming in. I'd like to hide in the observation room for those interviews."

"No can do, Moon. I have those gals from the wrestling league coming in back-to-back all day tomorrow. Tell you what, I'll have Deputy Johnson record the interviews, and you can stop by after hours and review the tapes."

A wave of self-doubt hits me. "I don't know if I can pick stuff up from videotape. I usually listen to the interviews live, and that's how I get my vibes."

Grams blurts to my rescue. "Have some faith in yourself, sweetie. This would be a good test of your abilities. You know you're getting better at managing things every day. But you can always call Silas for a little extra confidence booster."

"Good idea."

Erick scrunches up his face in confusion. "I feel like I missed something."

"Sorry. Grams thinks I can do it, but she suggested talking to Silas to find out if there's any additional things I can try."

"Got it. Are you ready to order that pizza?"

My face flushes. "Did you hear my stomach growl, or are you just hungry?"

He glances across the coffee table at me and winks. "I'm famished."

Hello! Tummy tingles.

Grabbing my phone, I walk away from Sheriff Too-Hot-To-Handle and place my pizza order.

Grams writes out new cards for Raelyn, Cobb, and for the manila rope.

Here's hoping one of these leads will pan out and point us in the right direction. Finding the killer will never make up for losing Tanya, but at least it will give everyone who cared about her some kind of closure.

CHAPTER 13

By the time daylight has seeped into my room and pried my eyes open, it's nearly midday! I have no memory of Erick leaving for work, and he must've taken the liberty of feeding the fiendish feline. I can assure you if Pyewacket was still sans Fruity Puffs, a large paw thwacking me upside the head would've done the job of daylight hours ago.

Rolling over, I hit the button to raise the blackout shades and attempt to launch out from beneath the thick winter comforter in one smooth move.

I think we all know what happens next ...

My smooth move becomes a tangled web, and my top half reaches freedom long before my feet.

Fortunately, I don't have far to fall, and there are no witnesses.

As I toss pillows, blankets, and a thick comforter back onto the bed, a strange plushy owl catches my eye. Looks like something from the items stacked in the children's literature section. Pye probably dragged it up here in some hunting fantasy. I'll take it back downstairs later.

Keeping with the casual tone of the morning, I slip into my robe and wander the great distance from the antique four-poster bed to the overstuffed settee before calling my alchemical mentor.

"Good morning, Mr. Willoughby. How do you fare on this fine day?" He's nothing if not a stickler for manners. I'm taking no chances.

"Mizithra! It is most fortuitous that you've called. I'm treating myself to an early lunch at the diner. Would you care to join me?"

I want to shout, "Would I? Hot damn, I'll be there in five!" But I've learned to control my baser impulses during my residency in Pin Cherry. "That sounds lovely. I'll see you in about five minutes."

"Wonderful. Good day."

The call ends, and I shake my head and chuckle.

Before arriving in Pin Cherry Harbor, I almost never used my cell to place phone calls. When I could actually afford to pay for service, 99.9% of my communications were via text. However, now that I've gotten into more of a habit of calling people and tuning my abilities to their vocal intonations, I've learned to appreciate the finer points of phone etiquette. And if I ever forget, the irascible Silas Willoughby is only too eager to remind me.

It barely takes a minute to splash some cold water on my face, throw on some protective lip balm, and rake my fingers through my haystack of hair. Skinny jeans shoved into winter boots and a T-shirt finish my uncomplicated ensemble. Choosing a T-shirt in this weather is risky, but my jacket claims to be tested at Arctic temperatures, so I hope to survive the brief walk to the diner.

Today's T-shirt should bring a smile, if not a full-blown snicker, from Mr. Willoughby. A grouchy cat stares through slits for eyes, and beneath him, the tagline reads, "I fully intend to haunt people when I die. I have a list."

The diner is bustling, and for a moment, I'm concerned I've forgotten one of Pin Cherry Harbor's famous festivals. Better check with the expert.

"Hey, Silas. Why is it so crowded?"

He harrumphs and smooths his bushy grey mustache with a thumb and forefinger. "Contrary to your assumptions, I am not an ambassador for the Chamber of Commerce. Perhaps the unseasonable warmth has drawn the city dwellers north."

Unzipping my jacket, but leaving it on for self-preservation, I slide onto the bench seat. "You call this unseasonable warmth? Unseasonable warmth is one hundred and five, in May, in the high desert. I'd categorize today's local weather as barely survivable."

Silas grins, catches sight of my shirt, and laughs until his jowly cheeks turn red, and a tear leaks from the corner of his eye.

A satisfied grin spreads across my face. "Wow! The shirt was a bigger hit than I thought. Why is that?" I'm immediately suspicious.

"I suppose I was reflecting on Isadora. Part of the reason I labored tirelessly to ensure her spirit was tethered to the bookshop was to prevent her ticking off names on just such a list."

Shock grips my features, followed by uncontrollable giggles.

Odell approaches our table with an egg-white omelette and a side of fruit for Silas, and a juicy cheeseburger with an enormous side of french fries for me.

"You know what, Gramps? You're my favorite relative. For reals. My absolute, cross my heart hope to die, favorite."

He sniffs sharply, grins despite himself, and raps his knuckles twice on the Formica tabletop.

"What was the impetus for your call this morning?" Silas takes an extra napkin and tucks it over his ancient bowtie.

Normally I'd serve up a reply through my mouth full of fries, but Silas would never stand for such crass behavior. I finish chewing, swallow my food, and even wipe my mouth with a thin paper napkin before I reply. "Yeah, I got so excited about the possibility of fries I completely forgot the original purpose of my mission."

My mentor's rheumy blue eyes instantly sharpen. "Mission? How long do I have to prepare?"

"Hopefully, you won't need any time at all. I was sort of hoping you'd come back to the bookshop with me, and we can get it all sorted out there. I need to get vibes off of a videotape, and I have no clue."

Silas carefully cuts a bite of his omelette, chews slowly, and swallows. After a long sip of java and a proper napkin dabbing of his mustache, his face contorts in utter confusion. "I must admit, the jargon of the youth escapes me. Is Vibes off of a Videotape a new rock 'n' roll band you prefer?"

It takes every bit of self-control I don't possess not to laugh out loud. Instead, I clear my throat loudly to cover the chuckles. "No. Not at all. I'm running an undercover operation as a female wrestler, so it's not really safe for me to hang out at the sheriff's station while Erick questions the rest of the wrestlers. Deputy Johnson is going to videotape the interviews, and I'm supposed to head over after hours to watch the tapes. But I don't really know how to pick up information off of a videotape. I was hoping you'd give me some pointers. I know there's gotta be something I can do to help move this investigation along and bring Tanya's murderer to justice."

Silas nods solemnly and reaches inside his tattered tweed coat.

I've seen him pull all manner of surprises from that fusty old jacket, so I find myself holding my breath.

No joy. It's only a handkerchief.

He swipes at his nose, replaces the kerchief, and smiles briefly. "I shall assist in any way I can. Do you remember the method I taught you for passive acquisition?"

I'm not even sure what passive acquisition might refer to, but I warrant a guess. "Is it that catcher's mitt thing?"

He smiles brightly, as though I've solved the Double Jeopardy question. "Indeed. This exercise will be much the same — with a slight adjustment for technology. Once we complete our dining experience, we can retire to the Rare Books Loft and I shall give you some time to practice."

"Sounds good. I knew I could count on you."

He gazes at me with the most serious of expressions. "Of course. You may always rely on me, Mizithra. Always."

The somber tone in his voice raises the hairs on the back of my neck, and I struggle to swallow my perhaps oversized bite of cheeseburger.

Finishing my meal in the usual under ten minutes, I fill Silas in on my wrestling persona while he eats as daintily as a Victorian woman at a ladies' luncheon.

At long last, he finishes eating, and we walk the half-block to the bookstore.

Safely wrapped in the scent of old books and mystery, I pull out a chair and drag it to the oak reading table where Silas sits prim and proper.

"As always, you must clear your mind. Take several deep breaths. When you are in the presence of people, or animals, you are able to heighten your senses and extract information. Indeed, I have taught you techniques to extract information even from unwilling subjects. The feeling of the videotape will be completely different. You are viewing an event that has already occurred. No active searching or digging on your part can affect the outcome.

"Copy that. Are you gonna teach me how to time travel?"

"The intricacies of the time-space continuum

are not a matter for jocularity, Mizithra. Grave consequences can occur."

Oops. Formal name territory. Not only did he answer too quickly, but also his tone spoke of seriousness and experience. Best not to lift that stone. "I didn't mean to joke. I take our training sessions very seriously. Humor is my natural defense mechanism."

My words spark his interest, and he inhales sharply. "Against what must you defend yourself?"

"Seriously? You're kind of intimidating, Silas. I mean, I love you like a kooky uncle, but you can be a little judge-y."

Rather than taking offense, he chuckles lightly. "I am your mentor first, and your friend second. Now, you must sink within yourself and let your senses travel past the electronic interference. At first, you will feel nothing but the rush of the tape. You must not attempt to push through that. In fact, it would be best if you pull away, letting that noise fade into the background."

"All right. I can do that. And then what?"

He smooths his mustache, steeples his fingers, and bounces his chin on the tip of his pointer finger.

Oh brother. It's lesson time.

"What do you imagine would happen next?"

I've watched hours and hours of videotape. I may have dropped out of film school without completing my coursework, but I edited a heckuva lot of footage while I was there. Using my ability to replay memories as scenes in my mind, I go back to a lonely night in the editing bay.

It's five years in the past, and I'm scrubbing through footage of a zombie wedding. Don't ask. The two actors deliver their lines with the overzealous amateurishness of most poorly directed student films. However, as I float within the memory, I sense fear from the actress. Not stage fright. She has a genuine fear of the actor working opposite her in the scene. At the time, we all gossiped behind her back about what a diva she was and chalked it up to a bit of fame being dangerous.

Sinking deeper, I sense a predatory vibe from the actor. Holy Weinstein, Batman! I definitely missed that on the day.

Opening my eyes, I gaze at my mentor, and a sly grin has tugged up the corners of his mouth. "Tell me."

I relay the details that played out in my memory, and he smiles like a proud father. "Precisely the skill set you will need when you review the tapes. No preconceived notions. No expectations. Quiet. A desire to know, but not control."

"Thank you, Obi-Wan." Star Wars seems to be the one pop culture reference he's in tune with, so I risk the comment.

His eyelids lounge lazily, and he harrumphs. "I suppose that is enough for today."

"As always, thank you, Mr. Willoughby."

When I stand to move my chair back to its appointed reading table, a flash of tan fur rockets across the loft.

Pyewacket leaps onto the table in front of Silas, drops something, and launches to the floor. He races along one narrow curved arm of the mezzanine that encircles the stacks below. Once out of sight, he coughs and hacks dangerously.

"Do you think Pye is all right? Should I take him to the vet?"

Silas points to the object on the desk. "I fear our intrepid messenger has a great dislike for tobacco."

Staring at the cigar, I shrug helplessly. "What the heck is that?"

He reaches out with his left hand and inspects the object thoroughly. "I believe it is a six-inch Corona with a 42 ring gauge."

"No, Silas. I know it's a cigar. But Pyewacket usually brings clues. What kind of clue is that? Does the murderer smoke cigars?"

Silas rises with a groan and a lengthy exhale. He picks up the cigar and tucks it into one of the many hidden pockets within his coat. "Sometimes, Mizithra, a cigar is just a cigar."

CHAPTER 14

Yeesh! Silas and his esoteric jokes. Once he clears out, I strongly consider selecting one of the many titles in my bookshop and settling in for a lazy afternoon of reading. However, an unexpected text arrives from Sheriff Harper.

"The wrestlers came in batches. Done way sooner than expected. Even finished questioning Cobb. Head over anytime you like."

Wow. All business. No sass and no kissy-face emoji. Whatevs.

Who knows how many hours of tape I'll have to scrub through. Might as well get started.

Stepping into the apartment, I bundle up for my march down Main Street.

When I enter the plain brick building, the sheriff's station's front desk is abandoned. No skin off my nose. This is practically my second home.

I meander through the equally empty bullpen and saunter into Erick's office. "Howdy, pardner. Cherry Darling reportin' for duty."

He seems unamused by my accent and my performance. "I hate to put all my eggs in one basket, Moon. But, as of right now, this entire investigation is resting on you getting one of your *hunches*. Also, the wrestler called Hallucna Jenn refused to give us her real name. So if you get any vibes on that, let me know."

His broad shoulders sag under the weight of a potentially unsolved murder. It's my psychic girl-friend duty to somehow lighten the load. "Don't worry, Sheriff, I got you."

He leads me across the hall to the observation room and sets up the tape. I'm happy to report it's just one tape. This should be a breeze for an old pro like me. Erick shows me the rudimentary controls for fast-forward, rewind, and pause, then leaves me to my own devices.

Just when I'm about to throw a tiny pity party, he returns with a bag of potato chips and a can of soda, or, as they call it at this latitude, "pop."

"Thanks, Erick. I was beginning to feel under-appreciated."

He puts two hands on the back of my chair,

leans down close, and speaks hotly to the back of my neck. "Don't worry, Moon. I've only begun to show you how much I appreciate you."

And, I'm dead.

"Erick! You better get out of here. I have actual work to do."

He chuckles in that deep, gravelly, sexy way, and strides out of the observation room.

The first interview is with Holly Hitter. I haven't really gotten to know her, so I pretty much watch the entire interview at regular speed. Nothing much to glean from her monosyllabic answers. Although, it may be worth noting that she's one of the ex-cons on the team and is currently in some court-mandated anger-management program. The juxtaposition of anger management and full-on women's wrestling makes me giggle too loudly in the quiet room.

The next couple of interviews are equally uneventful, and then we get to Raelyn, a.k.a. Anna Mel Cracker. Interestingly, she drops Cobb's name and his employer after only a couple of questions. Sinking into my Tootsie-pop center, I sense she has a genuine fear of the man. Maybe giving him up so easily is her last-ditch cry for help.

She doesn't shed much new light on things, but she does mention seeing a therapist as part of her requirements to transition from the halfway house to total independence.

A'dealya Payne takes a different approach in her interview. She's snarky, aggressive, and doesn't give up anything. On the surface, she seems way too defensive and possibly guilty of something.

However, when I sink into the calm place that allows me to receive additional information, I quickly discover the snark and anger are defense mechanisms. She's deeply scarred by an unnamed trauma. She'd potentially do anything to keep from getting hurt again.

Great. Another name to add to my probably-not-guilty list.

Anita Gurney is overly helpful. She's completed all requirements, transitioned to life on her own, and considers herself somewhat of an expert on thriving post-abuse. She answers every question Erick asks. The only new piece of information she has is regarding some new legal case Tanya was working.

Despite her earlier cooperation, at this point in the interview, she digs her heels in and insists that she can't give Erick the name of Tanya's client. That she only knows about it because the client is a close friend. She claims revealing that would be un-ethical and may put her friend in danger.

Pausing the tape, I close my eyes and think back

to who might be her close friend. I remember seeing her hanging out with Hallucna Jenn before and after the match. And they sat next to each other when we went out for drinks after practice.

I pull my senses to hyper-focus and fast-forward to Hallucna Jenn's interview.

She seems more cagey in the interview than she does in the ring — if that's even possible. She partially answers each question, but her voice tends to trail off in the middle of the sentence, and she ends with a shrug or a glance toward the floor. When Erick specifically mentions how important her help would be in finding Tanya's murderer, my psychic senses receive an icy jolt.

Hallucna Jenn is absolutely hiding something. I know she can be violent, but I can't imagine —

Erick has added some questions to his list after the previous interviews. He specifically questions her about therapy.

Every fiber of her being sharpens like the raised quills on a porcupine. She mumbles an answer, but her words aren't important to me.

I feel the truth. She *is* in therapy, but there's something off about the therapist. Hallucna Jenn doesn't fully trust her. I suppose trust issues are common among victims of abuse, but there's something more . . .

Fast forwarding through the next couple of

wrestlers, I finally get to the interview with Cobb Astley.

He sits with his arms crossed and his teeth clenched. Clearly, this guy isn't going to give up anything without a fight.

Erick takes a surprising approach. Generally, he's subtle and works like a surgeon with a scalpel. For lack of a better analogy, he attacks this interview in the style of his girlfriend, Mitzy Moon. From left field.

"Why were you attempting to strangle your girlfriend in the parking lot before the wrestling match, Mr. Astley?"

A series of emotions flash across the large man's bearded face. Shock. Fear. Suspicion. Anger. "Did that ditzy blonde report me?"

Rude.

Erick ignores the attack on my person. "I happened to attend the match, Mr. Astley. You didn't answer my question."

Cobb fidgets in his chair, crosses and uncrosses his arms, and swallows audibly. "We had a disagreement. Me and my ol' lady don't see eye to eye on everything. She thinks she hasta take care of all those chicks on the team. I think that's bull —"

"Language, Mr. Astley." Erick follows the warning with a shake of his head.

Cobb adjusts himself in his chair and puts his

hands in his lap. "Yeah. Fine. Anyway, she tries to manage all their lives, but she can't even keep track of her own. I tell her to stop being so overbearing, but she doesn't listen. You know?"

"And you thought putting your hands around her throat would help her hearing?"

Mr. Astley throws his arms in the air and exhales loudly. "Look, Sheriff, it was a misunderstanding. We're square. Nothing happened. No one was hurt. Whaddya want me to say?"

Erick lowers his voice to a threatening gravelly whisper and leans toward Cobb. "I want you to say it will never happen again. Ever. You got me?"

The expression on Cobb's face doesn't change, but the wave of fear and respect that hits my psychic senses is unmistakable. Astley opens and closes his mouth a couple of times before he lands on the right response. "Understood, Sheriff, sir."

With that, Erick confirms that Cobb works at the marina and has access to manila rope. However, Cobb swears he hasn't seen Tanya since the safe house incident last year. The sheriff releases Mr. Astley, and we come to the end of the interviews. I stop the tape and turn off the machine.

As I lean back in my chair, munching on my remaining potato chips, a sudden assist from my extrasensory perceptions finally blasts through the fog.

"Therapy!"

I pull my feet off the narrow desk, open the door, and barge into Erick's office.

When I say barge, I mean it. The door was closed, and I didn't even knock.

He spins, his bare, broad chest in full view, with his blue jeans unzipped.

Clearly, I interrupted a superhero changing in a phone booth moment. "Sorry! I'm so sorry! I —"

"Moon, can you close the door?"

"Yes. Of course. Sorry." I close the door, lean against it and attempt to catch my breath. Not that the sight of him half-dressed is unwelcome, but it was highly unexpected. And, as usual, has sent my heart all aflutter.

He grins and basks in my embarrassment. "Was there something I could help you with?"

Swallowing tightly, I drag my eyes from his abs up to his mischievous blue eyes. "There was — I came in to — Can you put a shirt on?"

He chuckles wickedly and finishes getting dressed. "Better?"

"For now."

"What's the big news? Did you crack the case?"

"Maybe. Maybe not. But I definitely have a lead. Several of the women mentioned therapy. It stands to reason there aren't a ton of therapists willing to work pro bono or on a sliding scale.

There's a super good chance they're all going to the same therapist. I don't know if that connection means anything or if it goes anywhere, but I'm gonna head over to Pilar's house and see if she can give me a name."

Erick nods. "That's good. That could definitely be something. I'm finished here. I'll come with you."

Smiling at him as though he's a silly child, I shake my head. "Hey, right from the beginning, Pilar said there were things she could tell me that you absolutely could not know. I'm not sure this therapist thing would be one of them, but I definitely think I better go alone. Don't worry, you'll be my first phone call."

He exhales, and his shoulders return to their sagging disappointment. "Fine. I'll grab some chow at the diner and hang out there until I get your call."

"Say hi to Odell for me. I won't be long."

Distracted with the zipper on my jacket, I fail to notice Erick close the distance between us. When I look up, his arms encircle me, and he pulls me tightly against him. "It was rough to talk to all of those women today. A lot of them have been through hell. I would never treat you like that." His voice cracks and my heart breaks a little.

"I know. I know. You would never treat anyone like that. I mean, thank you for saying that, but I know you're a good person, Erick. Better than good. You're a great person."

His lips are on mine in an instant, and all the worries of the day evaporate with his kiss. As my knees begin to weaken, I'm forced to extract myself. "Hey, save some of that enthusiasm for later. I've got to get over to Pilar's. I know she has a couple of kids, and I don't know what bedtime routines or whatever they've got going on over there. I'll text you as soon as I leave. All right?"

His breathing is heavy, and I can sense the increase in his heart rate. "Yeah. Sounds good. Catch you later."

His offhand comment fools no one.

I've still got it!

CHAPTER 15

A QUICK TEXT to Pilar gives me permission for another visit. They live in an area of Pin Cherry Harbor known as The Pines. Apparently, dry cleaning is a lucrative business. I've always been told that The Pines is considered the posh part of town.

Pilar meets me at the door and ushers me into their warm, bustling kitchen. This time the children are home.

"Hey, guys, this is Mitzy Moon. Mitzy, this is our daughter Lilith, and that's her brother McKenzie playing video games."

Lilith sits at the table, powering through a large bowl of stir-fry. Her mouth is full, but she grins and waves brightly. McKenzie offers zero recognition of my arrival.

"Hi, Lilith. Nice to meet you. Mind if I steal your mom away for a minute or two?"

Lilith gulps down her bite of food. "No problem. Gotta get to hockey practice."

My eyes widen in surprise, and I glance at Pilar.

"Lilith, you have to get in at least thirty minutes of cello practice before your ride gets here."

"Awwwww, Mom!"

"No discussion. Dish up your brother's food, and then hustle upstairs to practice."

Lilith fails to acknowledge her mother's request. "Mac! You cool?"

Reminding me of Deputy Baird down at the precinct, Mac does not take his eyes off the screen. "Yeah, I'm cool."

"Mom, Mac is cool."

Pilar exhales and rolls her eyes. "Fine. Then get upstairs and get that cello practice in before your ride gets here."

She puts her arm around my shoulders and leads me into a cozy reading nook at the very front of the house. As soon as we're alone, she blurts, "I haven't told them." Her eyes instantly brim with tears.

Leaning toward her, I lower my voice. "Seriously? Where do they think Tanya is?"

Pilar sighs and shrugs. "She has to travel sometimes. I made up a little white lie about her having a business conference. I just can't —" She presses a hand to her mouth, and silent tears trickle down her cheeks.

As if on cue, the haunting notes of the cello tumble down the stairs.

Rather than jumping in and pretending to know the first thing about parenting, I take a deep breath and rely on my other senses. She's exhausted. She's heartbroken. She's holding everything together by the very thinnest of threads.

"Look, Pilar, no judgment. I don't know anything about raising children. But you're going to have to tell them at some point."

She grips my arm for support, draws a ragged breath, and nods. "I was hoping to wait until the case was solved. At least then, I can tell them that there'll be some justice for their mother. I can't bear to tell them we don't even know what happened. That no one's being held responsible. I can't do that."

Her logic does make sense. "I get it. I'm doing everything I can. In fact, that's why I'm here. There's a connection between all the ladies in the wrestling league. Well, maybe not all of them, but a lot of them. Therapy seems to be an important part of their recovery. Whether it's part of transitioning or post-trauma care, or whatever . . . I'm no psychologist. Anyway, it occurred to me they might all be seeing the same person. I need to know who that person is. Do you have any idea?"

Pilar utters an enormous sigh of relief. "Oh, gosh. I thought you had some terrible news. They all see Dr. Maggie Mareno. She's a great psychiatrist. Some of the women need to be on medication, and that allows her to run the therapy sessions and issue prescriptions. She's extremely fair with her billing practices. Maggie takes a few pro bono cases and puts the rest on a sliding scale. Generally, the women's shelter has a budget to cover several sessions. Tanya works all sorts of deals to cover the rest."

"That's great. I really need to talk to this Maggie Mareno, though. Do you think it's all right if I give her a call?"

"No problem. It's a little too late to call her tonight, but give her a buzz tomorrow and let her know you're working on Tanya's —" Pilar claps a hand over her mouth and blinks back tears.

"I'll do that." My heart goes out to this wonderful woman working so hard to protect her children. "Hey, do you need a hug?"

A strangled moan escapes from Pilar's chest, and she nods.

"By the way, how's Cornwell doing? Is she gonna recover from that crusher gone wrong?"

A weak smile lifts Pilar's cheeks. "Yes. Thank

goodness. I can't handle any more bad news right now." She sighs.

I offer her a comforting embrace. "I better hit the road. By the way, your daughter, Lilith, seems like a real pistol." I point to the ceiling. "And she can play the heck out of that cello."

For a moment, the tension fades from Pilar's face. "You have no idea. Some days I wonder how we —" Tears bubble to the corners of her eyes. "How we got so lucky. Lil is smart as a whip, determined as all get out, and so generous. When she gets back from hockey practice tonight, she's baking six-dozen cupcakes for a fundraiser for the animal shelter. I'll help her, of course. But that's our Lil." The moment she finishes the sentence, the weight of sadness returns.

"If there's ever anything I can do for you or your family, you let me know. The Duncan-Moon Foundation is eager to give back to the community. And you and your family are an important part of our community."

She sniffles and sighs. "Thank you. But — No. Wait. Tanya taught me to just say thank you and accept generosity. So, thank you. I'll let you know if anything comes up."

I offer her one more hug for the road and head toward the diner. I've opted to pop in and help myself to some chili cheese fries rather than simply send a text and risk Erick talking me out of an opportunity to indulge in golden, french-fried perfection.

WHEN I ENTER THE DINER, two of my favorite people are hunched toward each other in the corner booth. It seems I've interrupted a serious conversation between Erick and Odell. My hereditary snoop gene longs to dive in and get details. However, I've personally sworn an oath not to use my powers on Erick. Everyone is entitled to some privacy.

As I approach the booth, Odell slides off the bench seat and offers me a quick hug. "I'll drop a basket of fries down and have your order out in a flash, kid."

"Thanks, Gramps." I used to wonder how he always knew exactly what his regular patrons wanted before they even placed an order, but now that I've traced one of the roots of my family tree back to him, the precognizance seems quite normal.

When I slide into the booth, Erick waves his phone in my general direction. "I don't remember getting a text, Moon."

"Yeah, about that. I had a craving for chili cheese fries."

He chuckles and shakes his head. "No harm done. Any good news?"

"Absolutely. My hunch was spot on. They all see a psychiatrist named Dr. Maggie Mareno."

"I appreciate you getting the info. I'll have to bring Dr. Mareno in for an official interview."

Initially, I bristle at his interference, but the practical side of my brain reminds me that he is the actual sheriff. "Copy that. Can I at least —"

"Sneak into the observation room and eavesdrop on my interview?"

"You're not wrong."

He walks his fingers across the table and turns his palm up. As I slide my hand into his, he rubs his thumb along my fingers and grins. "Of course you can. But try not to let Deputy Paulsen see you. Okay?"

"10-4, Sheriff."

Odell arrives with my gorgeous plate of chili cheese fries in one hand and the coffeepot in the other. He slides my delectable treat onto the table.

The aroma of spicy chili and melted cheese fills my nostrils. "As wonderful as I had hoped."

Odell refills Erick's coffee, raps his knuckles twice on the table, and returns to the kitchen to give us some privacy.

Gosh darn it, I love that man.

Erick removes a notepad from the pocket of his jacket and jots down a couple of things while I dig into my feast. He smirks across the table and winks. "Maybe I should do the talking for a couple of minutes while you work your way through that."

My mouth is extremely full, and even my usual lack of manners doesn't allow me to respond.

He seems pleased by that result. "We finally got a warrant approved for Tanya's office."

My eyes widen, and I lift a finger.

He shakes his head. "You don't have to ask. She had a separate little law office she rented. Nothing official, just somewhere to meet clients and keep records. I'm hoping we can serve the warrant tomorrow and get the deputies started going through the files."

I nod vigorously.

"Hopefully, something will turn up. After talking to all of those women, I don't think a single one of them could possibly be guilty of this homicide. But I'm not ruling out the possibility of one of them having a connection to the actual murderer." He lifts his mug in a halfhearted toast. "Here's hoping."

Wiping my mouth with a thin paper napkin, I lift a forkful of chili cheese fries and grin. "I'll second that."

As soon as I finish my scrumptious snack, we head back to the bookshop. Grams is hard at work at the desk in the corner of my apartment. Usually, there's no problem with her working in the apartment, but tonight I'm entertaining.

"Hey, Grams, can we get a little privacy?"

Erick glances around the room, attempting to follow my gaze to the location of a ghost he barely believes in and definitely can't see.

Her translucent head spins, and she looks at me in confusion. "Oh, Mitzy. I was so engrossed in my edits I didn't even hear you come home. What did you say?"

Jerking a thumb over my shoulder toward Erick, I wink and repeat myself. "I was hoping for some alone time with my fiancé."

Ghost-ma hastily drops her quill pen and zooms toward me. "Of course, sweetie. Tell Erick I like those jeans."

I send her a curt telepathic message. *I will do no such thing.*

She giggles like a schoolgirl and vanishes through the wall.

Erick cautiously approaches. "So, are we alone?"

"Yes. We have the apartment to ourselves."

No sooner have I made my bold statement than a wily caracal saunters from the closet.

"Well, looks like we'll be sharing it with Pyewacket."

Erick crouches and reaches toward the furry fiend.

I'm happy to say Pye completely ignores him. He slinks toward the murder board, rises on his hind legs, and thwacks the cork firmly.

"Yes, your royal furriness. We do have an update for the murder board. Tomorrow Erick will be questioning a psychiatrist named Maggie Mareno. I'll let Grams make up the card for her in the morning. Satisfied?"

Rather than his usual intonation, he offers me a sharp warning, and somehow the word *cigar* floats through the air.

"What is it with you and that cigar?"

My confused boyfriend looks at me and shrugs. "I don't see a cigar. Is it a ghost thing?"

I fill him in on Pyewacket's earlier delivery, the one usurped by Silas, and even repeat the joke from my mentor. "And then he said, sometimes a cigar is just a cigar."

Erick smiles quickly and nods his head appreciatively toward Pye.

I'm not fond of being left out. "What's going on? What's happening with you two?"

He stands, crosses his arms, and exhales dramatically. "That cat really is a genius."

Throwing my hands in the air, I scoff. "Could

you please fill me in? I'm totally on the outside here."

Erick tilts his head and nods. "I know exactly how that feels, Moon."

"Touché." I make no attempt to hide my eye roll.

"That line, sometimes a cigar is just a cigar, is always attributed to Sigmund Freud. I believe he's considered by some to be the father of modern psychiatric medicine."

The pieces flip into place like a perfect game of Tetris. "Yeesh! My extra sensory stuff must've been on the fritz. All the books about relationships, trying to steal the ring . . ."

Bowing to my entitled fur baby, I reverently whisper, "Pyewacket, some days I feel I don't deserve your genius. Mad respect, son."

"Reow." Can confirm.

CHAPTER 16

MY LAZY MORNING lounging around the apartment is wearing thin. I need that text from Erick to set things in motion.

Pyewacket seems to be over it as well. I toss a bit of sausage from the leftover cold pizza his direction, and, rather than leaping high into the air to snatch it in mid-flight, he flops lazily onto his belly and basically Army-crawls close enough to grasp it with his sharp teeth.

"I feel you, buddy. If he doesn't text —"

PING.

"Dr. Mareno here soon."

Now that the day has a hint of hope, I find the energy to wash my face and get dressed.

Wandering downstairs, I brew a second pot of

coffee. Twiggy is coming in late today because she has to take her dogs to the vet. Hopefully, everything's all right. Bartels and Jaymes are two of the cutest pups I've met since I arrived in town. I'm sure it's nothing serious, and I know Twiggy will appreciate the java.

I could head to the diner and continue my lazy morning of snacking, but I'd really rather —

PING.

"The psychiatrist arrived. On your way?"

That's my guy! I tap out a hasty reply to Erick's text. "You betcha!" One of the many local colloquialisms I've come to enjoy.

I'm pleased to report no one stands between me and hiding out in the observation room. If they were successful in serving the warrant at Tanya's side-hustle office this morning, it stands to reason all the deputies are busy combing through the confiscated files.

I take a seat and flip the silver toggle on the speaker below the one-way glass window.

Erick is close to finishing up the basics — confirming her name, address, and profession.

Rubbing my hands together eagerly, I await the meat of the interview.

"Thank you for coming in today, Dr. Mareno."

"Of course. I am always happy to help out Birch County's finest."

"I understand you treat several of the women from the shelter at your practice in Broken Rock. Is that correct?"

She nods vigorously.

"Please answer verbally for the recording."

"Oh, of course. Yes, that is correct."

"Are you acquainted with the local lawyer Tanya Tucker?"

"Yes. I used to have a large mental health practice in Chicago, but the stress of big-city living took its toll. I sold my practice and moved as far north as I could. Landing in Broken Rock has been a godsend. The pace is slower, my practice is smaller, and my heart is fuller."

"And this is when you met Ms. Tucker?"

"Oh, sorry. I got lost in my own story. Ms. Tucker found me. She was looking for a psychiatrist who would be willing to take a few pro bono cases and offer a reasonable sliding scale to traumatized women working hard to transition to a new life. I made a nice profit on the sale of my practice, and once I heard Tanya's sales pitch, I was all in. Happy to give back."

"And do you have issues with any of the women?"

"Issues? I'm not sure I understand the question, Sheriff." Maggie tilts her head, and her salt and pepper curls fall to the left as she adjusts her glasses.

Erick slides his hands along the edge of the table and leans back. "It's my understanding that some of these women are ex-convicts looking to transition from halfway houses to independent lives. Have there been any instances of violence?"

The super cooperative woman hesitates for a split second, and her nostrils flare. Although everything seems to be fine, when a large smile lifts her full cheeks. "Well, sometimes the women become agitated when talking about past traumas or mistakes that led to their current situations. However, I have never had any of them become violent in a session."

My mood ring burns with a message, and I glance at my left hand in time to see an image of Cobb squeezing his hands around Raelyn's throat. Should I interrupt the interview? I'm not exactly sure what the message means, but maybe I'm supposed to share with Erick.

Sheriff Harper shuffles through some papers on the table and clears his throat. "Understood. Can you confirm you're seeing Raelyn Engle?"

Maggie wrings her hands and sets them tentatively on the table. "We are venturing into a sensitive area, Sheriff. I have an obligation to protect patient privacy. Can you perhaps rephrase?"

My brilliant boyfriend sees the obstacle and immediately hurdles over it. "In my interview with Raelyn Engle, she mentioned seeing a therapist. Would you be that therapist?"

Maggie grins nervously. "I'm comfortable confirming that, Sheriff."

"Thank you." He moves the papers again, and something tells me he's going on a fishing trip with no bait and pretty low expectations. "Dr. Mareno, Raelyn mentioned an incident before the wrestling match this past Saturday. Cobb Astley had his hands around her throat, and, by every indication, she feared for her safety. Has she reported any similar incidents to you in the past?"

"I'm not at liberty to give you specific details, but I can confirm similar incidents have been reported." The woman shifts nervously in her chair, and I sense discomfort. Although I'm not sure if the discomfort is related to treading the fine line of doctor-patient confidentiality or something deeper.

"The department is looking for connections between the women closest to Ms. Tucker and people from their past, or potentially current, situations that may be prone to this type of violence. Do you, in your medical opinion, think Mr. Astley is capable of murder?"

A strange energy washes over Dr. Mareno. She

seems intrigued with the question but not eager to answer. Weird.

"I've never met Mr. Astley, so it would be unprofessional of me to guess."

Erick exhales in frustration. "I'm not asking you to guess, Dr. Mareno. I'm asking for you to evaluate the reports your client has given you and make an educated judgment. Is Mr. Cobb capable of this type of violence?"

"I can't be sure, Sheriff. None of us can ever be sure. But I can tell you he has a terrible temper."

"I appreciate your professional input, Dr. Mareno. There may be —"

The interview is interrupted — not by me — by a knock on the door.

"Please excuse me for a moment, Dr. Mareno."

Erick rises from the chair and opens the door. I can clearly see Deputy Paulsen, but she says nothing. She shows Erick a piece of paper, and I instantly feel his energy shift. A moment ago, he felt like the end of a long exhale. The energy had slowly seeped out of him, and he had once again found himself without a solid lead.

No more. Whatever is on that piece of paper is a game changer.

He nods at Paulsen and closes the door. Without returning to his seat, he thanks the psychiatrist a second time and dismisses her with a note that they may need to speak to her again and that she should certainly feel free to call him if she thinks of any other individuals her clients have mentioned.

I basically have two speeds, snooping or dead asleep. I can't sit still. Barely able to wait a count of five, I rocket across the hallway and find Erick's office empty.

Blerg! I need to know what was on that piece of paper!

Spinning on the thick heel of my winter boot, I smash smack dab into the incredibly firm chest of Sheriff Harper.

"Where you headed in such a hurry, Moon?" His low chuckle sends my tummy into freefall.

An instant snark-shield will save me. "Hilarious. I'm laughing on the inside, Sheriff. I know there was something I need to see on that piece of paper. Don't make me use my special powers." I narrow my gaze and lean toward him in a false threat.

He lovingly plays along. Raising his hands in the air, he widens his eyes in mock horror. "No. Say it isn't so." Erick kisses my forehead, scoots past me, and drops into his badly abused office chair.

Reluctantly, I follow suit and plunk onto an unwelcoming visitor's chair. "Dish."

The sheriff chuckles. "It's absolutely nothing solid."

"I don't care if it's freaking jelly, Harper. Give me the deets!"

He smacks his lips expectantly and leans forward. "The deputies found something interesting when they were going through Tanya's papers this morning."

Ah ha! I knew the deputies were busy with those papers. "Go on."

"It doesn't look like it was an official case. There were no filings, but there were some brief notes about a potential conflict of interest. One of Dr. Mareno's female patients had claimed she was also treating the woman's ex-husband. A known threat."

"What? Why would a psychiatrist do that? What if they ran into each other in the waiting room?"

"Apparently, Dr. Mareno has a unique office layout. She occupies one wing of a much larger ranch-style building in Broken Rock, surrounded by a generous parking lot. She has a separate front entrance for patients checking in, and they leave through a different rear door from her office. Never crossing paths. It still seems like a breach to assume that she could treat both the wife and her accused abuser and risk them not running into each other."

"Heck yeah. Was Tanya planning on bringing some sort of malpractice lawsuit?"

"The notes indicated plans to have a chat with Dr. Mareno about the suspicion. That's where it ends. There was no confirmation, no further action. Problem is, she doesn't name the woman on whose behalf she was working. We'd have to bring in every single one of the wrestlers again and see if one of them will admit to the suspicions. That could easily take another day or two. Any ideas?" His big blue eyes lock onto me with desperate hope.

"Remember how I told you I got a weird vibe when you were questioning Hallucna Jenn. Like, somehow, she didn't fully trust her therapist. Let's see if I can work my magic at practice this afternoon. If she's the one with the suspicions, I'll figure it out."

All I hear is a loud sigh of relief. "I don't care what Paulsen says. You're the best thing that ever happened to this department."

"Is she still causing trouble for you? You want me to talk to her? I'll go toe-to-toe with her in a second. No problem."

"Honestly, Moon, it's probably best if you do everything in your power to avoid Deputy Paulsen." He pops up from his chair, rounds the desk, and pulls me close. "I believe in you, Cherry. Knock 'em dead at practice."

Leaning into his embrace, I fan myself, throw on my best southern accent, and declare, "Oh, my."

His laughter follows me through the bullpen as I exit the station and hope for success at practice.

And not wrestling success. Psychic success.

CHAPTER 17

THE TURNOUT AT PRACTICE IS ABYSMAL. Apparently, Dylan Bernard has put through yet another injunction. Something about safety violations, citing the accident at our recent match. Holly Hitter swears the bolts were loosened, and the whole thing is a set up.

An icy chill encircles my ring finger, and a quick glance at the smoky cabochon reveals a brief flash of Cobb Astley's angry face. Suspicion confirmed. He has to be moonlighting for Dylan Bernard, and he definitely loosened those bolts. No wonder Anna Mel was so upset and threatening to spill the beans. She'd never want to intentionally hurt another wrestler. I'll have to mention this to Erick later.

Without the steadying reassurance of Pilar, the women are getting frustrated and jumping ship.

Lady luck, however, smiles down on me. Hallucna Jenn is in attendance. We get in a couple of good workout sessions, and she teaches me a move called the figure-four leg lock. It's not difficult to do, but it's terrifying to be locked in. It's one of those moves that can cause serious damage if you don't get out of it immediately.

The last of the die-hard wrestlers finally call it a day, and the hall at the fairgrounds is emptying fast.

Accent intact, I attempt to prolong my time with Hallucna Jenn. "Hey, y'all wanna grab a bite after practice?"

She eyes me with concern. "I don't need friends."

"Fine by me, missy. I just don't fancy eatin' alone. I'll pick up the tab if you provide the company."

Visible relief floods across her face when I mention paying for our meal. "Sure. Whatever. I only got an hour before my shift starts at the Supermart."

"Then we better skedaddle."

Fortunately, I've learned the trick of bringing a change of clothes to practice. We both get swapped out of our outfits and into civilian attire, and I offer to follow her to the eatery of her choice. I don't really know my way around Broken Rock, and I don't want to take a chance on choosing somewhere she'd be uncomfortable.

It's a short drive from the fairgrounds, outside of town, to Broken Rock. The roads are clear, and the waxing moon is up early, bringing a silvery glow to the snow-covered fields.

Hallucna Jenn selects the same chicken-entrée-laden bar of our first team outing, but this time we're the only ones in attendance.

We place our orders and get beers. Once we're seated, she relaxes, and I toss out a softball starter question. "How long you been wrestlin'?"

She sets down her beverage and wipes her mouth with the back of her hand. "Only about six months. Before that, I was —" Her eyes widen, and she clams up.

"Hey, you don't have to worry about nothin' with me. These lips are locked up tighter than Fort Knox." It doesn't feel great to lie to her, but solving Tanya's murder is my top priority.

Hallucna Jenn takes a shallow breath, chews her bottom lip, and sighs. "I was in a bad relationship."

Now's my chance to demonstrate we share some common ground. "Ain't they the worst! I once had me a beau that was meaner than a cornered badger. It wasn't till my auntie hit him upside the head with a rolling pin that he left me alone."

She looks down at the table and picks at the chipping varnish. "We don't all have an auntie."

"Whatever happened to you, it ain't your fault, darlin'. Sometimes we get dealt a bad hand. Maybe you just didn't fold as soon as you shoulda. There ain't nothin' wrong with taking care of yourself now. You got that?"

Hallucna Jenn looks at me with genuine appreciation. "Yeah, I finally got it."

Now that I've built a little rapport, it's time to do some digging. I'll have to be gentle if I hope to keep her from closing up like a Venus flytrap. "I'm sure Tanya was a great help to you. Do you have anyone else you can rely on?"

She shrugs her strong, athletic shoulders. "I got a therapist. But, I don't know —"

"Sounds like you got some doubts about this therapist. What's up with him or her?"

Hallucna Jenn puts her elbows on the table, balls up her fists, and presses her forehead against her hands. "You're gonna think I'm crazy."

"I once entered a contest to catch a greased pig for a prize of nothing more than $25. You don't know crazy, darlin'."

"Okay. She's got this weird setup at her office, you know. You come in one door and then leave through a different door. So you never see her other clients. I suppose that's good."

"Seems all right. What's got your knickers in a bunch?"

"There were a few times — like more than three — that I swear I could smell my ex's cologne in her office. It's distinct. Very thick and cloying. Like sandalwood, but darker and sweeter at the same time. Not a smell I'll ever forget."

"You sure it wasn't some kind of incense or air freshener?"

"No way. No one would use that odor to make things better." She nearly spits the words across the table, and I can feel her conviction with all of my senses, including the extra ones.

"Did you tell her about the smell? This therapist woman?"

"Yeah. She tried to act all normal, like I was just having some sort of sense memory, but something seemed off. Then I felt like I couldn't really trust her. I thought she was hiding something."

"Did you tell Tanya?" I'm hoping she brings up the lawsuit, because I have no way of naturally shoehorning that into this conversation.

"Yeah. That's the thing about Tanya. She always believed us. No matter what our stories were, if we'd done wrong, or made bad choices, Tanya always gave us another chance. She believed me the second I told her. She made some notes and promised to talk to the doc. I thought maybe for once in my life things were gonna go my way." She drifts into silence, and I say what she's thinking.

"And then someone took Tanya from us."

A thick silence hangs over the table.

I wish I could tell her I'm doing everything in my power to bring Tanya's killer to justice, and I'm hoping to see that Dr. Mareno is investigated as well, but I've sort of pigeonholed myself into this Cherry Darling character.

"I better let you get to your shift at the Supermart. I don't wanna be the reason you get in any kind of trouble."

Hallucna Jenn looks across the table with a flicker of hope in her eyes. "My real name is Loraina Vashun. You can call me Raina. All my friends do."

"Thanks. I'd like that." I'm awash with guilt. All I can pray for is a speedy resolution to this case and a chance to redeem myself in Raina's eyes.

I haven't been able to think about the crime scene since that first day. The sight of Tanya's body always sends my stomach running. But on the drive back to Pin Cherry Harbor, for some reason, an instant replay memory washes over me, and I'm forced to pull to the side of the road.

This time, the victim is the least important part of the imagery. As I move down that hallway, the smell of chemicals and the feel of the plastic bags on the floor brushing against my leg seem more real than the day I actually walked through the site. Glancing at the scratch marks on the wall, something suddenly strikes me as completely out of place. Between two sets of scratch marks, one high and one low, hangs a macramé owl. There's a piece of driftwood at the top and bottom to keep the hanging straight. However, as I peer more closely at the imagery with all of my senses, I see two disturbing facts. 1. The owl is facing the wall. 2. There's a third set of scratch marks hidden behind its woven body.

Time to call Erick.

I put my favorite sheriff on speaker and bring him up to speed on everything I know, and a few things I suspect.

"I'll send a deputy over immediately to bag that owl and drive it directly to the lab. I think you may have found the murder weapon, Moon."

"I hope so. But if the killer was wearing gloves, like you suspected, there won't be any DNA on the fibers."

"Maybe not. First, we need to confirm if it's the murder weapon, then we cross our fingers and hope the lab finds something more."

"Here's hoping."

I finish my story about Loraina Vashun and let him know there was no logical way for me to push for the name of Raina's ex-husband, but now that we have her real name, Erick should be able to get some details.

"I'll see you later, Moon."

"Hold on! I can't believe I almost forgot to mention this. Cobb Astley is the one who loosened those bolts on the turnbuckle."

"Hard evidence?"

Blerg. "No. But I'm one hundred percent psychically sure. Plus, I'm also positive he did the deed at the request of the litigious Dylan Bernard."

Erick blows a raspberry. "I'm not saying I disagree with you, Moon. In fact, we're certain Cobb and Dylan have crossed paths at the marina. Mr. Bernard owns an ostentatious yacht." He exhales. "The problem is, I need proof that will hold up in court. I'll get Deputy Gilbert to do some digging."

He ends the call with a promise to let me know as soon as he finds something.

As I'm pulling into my garage and tucking the keys under the sun visor, my phone rings.

"That was fast! Got something on the ex-husband angle?"

"Got a name and a picture. Without some probable cause, I've got no reason to bring this guy in. Some handwritten notes left by Tanya aren't going to cut it. I'll have to stake out the place and hopefully catch him and Dr. Mareno red-handed."

"A stakeout?" The thrill in my voice must be evident.

"Look, Moon, I thought it was pretty clear when I said I'd handle the stakeout. It wasn't an invitation."

"Since when do I need an invitation?"

His chuckle warms my heart. "It would be completely unofficial."

"Absolutely. I'm just a girl, hanging out with a boy, who happens to be sitting in a sheriff's cruiser."

He exhales in defeat, and I know I've got him exactly where I want him.

First thing in the morning, we're staking out Dr. Maggie Mareno's office.

CHAPTER 18

THE STAKEOUT BEGINS like a scene from every great cop/buddy movie I've ever seen.

Erick picks me up with two large coffees, a bag of doughnuts, and a grin brightening his entire expression.

We arrive in Broken Rock thirty minutes before Dr. Mareno's office officially opens. The sheriff finds a strategic parking spot behind the row of dumpsters at this end of the complex.

Most people wouldn't give a police vehicle a second look, but we happen to know some of Dr. Mareno's clientele have a questionable past. Seeing an officer of the law could spook them, and we don't want anyone mentioning our presence to the good doctor.

By midmorning, much of the enthusiasm that came up with the sun is waning.

"Maybe we're barking up the wrong tree, Sheriff. We've seen three people go in, all women."

He chuckles and drags his thumb along his jawline.

"What? What did I say that's so funny?" Crossing my arms defiantly, I await his reply.

"As I may have mentioned on more than one occasion, Moon, patience is not your strong suit. Stakeouts in real life are nothing like the movies you're so fond of referencing. Sometimes days will go by before you bag your quarry. But you can't let your guard down. That one moment you decide to call it an early day or go grab lunch — that's exactly when the perp you're looking for shows up. So, we're gonna run this stakeout by my rules. We sit here until she closes up for the day, and if we don't have anything, we come back tomorrow. You and I both know even her best clients are likely only seeing her once a week." He leans back, and the smug grin that sits on his handsome face rubs me the wrong way.

"Can't we cut to the chase? I'll just go in there and ask her if she's seeing Loraina Vashun's ex-husband. Even if she doesn't answer, I'll be able to pull the information or at least get a vibe."

Erick nods his head as though I've come up

with a brilliant plan. "Okay, Moon. Let's say we go with that idea. When I get on the stand to testify, how will I describe this 'vibing' process to the jury?"

As you might imagine, his wisecrack leaves me speechless.

Rather than give me unlimited time to answer, he continues. "Right now, you have no idea what Maggie Mareno has done. Is she simply guilty of some unethical psychiatric practices? Or is she Tanya's murderer? People do crazy things when they're backed into a corner. If you walk in there and ask the one question that flips her trigger a second time, what makes you think she wouldn't dispatch you as quickly as she did Tanya?"

The hypothetical scene sends a deathly chill across my shoulders, and I hug my arms around myself for protection. "Fine. I didn't think it through. We'll run the stakeout by your rules, but I'm gonna have to use the bathroom sooner or later. Have you got a plan for that?"

He glances toward the opposite end of the sprawling business park. "I saw a laundromat at the other end when we pulled in. I'm thinking they probably have a bathroom in there."

Turning in my seat to give him full access to my shocked expression, I inhale sharply. "You *think*?

Erick Harper, are you telling me you've never actually been inside a laundromat?"

He shrugs dismissively but doesn't make eye contact.

"Oh, the sheltered life of Ricky Harper. Your mama did your laundry until you went to college, and then you brought it home on weekends, and I'm assuming they have some huge laundry facility in the Army? How am I doing?"

"Whether or not I've been in a laundromat hardly seems pertinent, Moon." He lifts his chin and stares fixedly at the psychiatrist's entrance.

"Oh, no. You don't get to sidestep the topic that easily."

He turns toward me but averts his gaze.

"Like you said, we have all the time in the world. We may as well use some of it discussing your lack of real-life experiences." I'm about to get to the peak of my gloating when a figure steps out of a mahogany metallic Porsche Cayenne Turbo GT and strides toward Dr. Mareno's front door.

Wordlessly pointing, my eyes widen as I gesture frantically.

Erick's head snaps toward the clinic. "What the —? Now I'm really confused."

"That guy doesn't look anything like the picture of Raina's ex, Erick. Maybe he's had plastic surgery to change his appearance so Hallucna Jenn wouldn't know he was closing in on her."

Despite the tense situation, he laughs. "Moon, this is not a movie. That guy is not the ex-husband. That's Dylan Bernard, the owner of the men's wrestling league."

"Plot twist!" I clap excitedly, as though I'm Ghost-ma. "Is that enough to get a warrant?"

Erick rubs his hands along the steering wheel and taps his thumb pensively. "We'll make a note of it and hang out a few more hours. I've got Deputy Johnson tracking down more particulars on Loraina's ex. To be clear, I pretty much went with your gut and ignored proper procedure for this op. It would've been smart to confirm whether the guy still owned property in the area and where he was employed before settling on a stakeout. If Johnson turns up some information that places Mr. Vashun in some other town, Paulsen will have a field day."

"Not if the connection between Dylan Bernard and Dr. Mareno proves to be as juicy as I think it's going to be."

Several hours and one trip to the laundromat restroom later, we have no additional hot tips.

Erick returns me to the bookshop and promises to text me in the morning, when he's got Dylan and Maggie in their separate interview rooms.

. . .

THE GLOW FROM THE OLD CRT SCREEN in the back room spills into the hallway. "Twiggy? Is that —?"

Before I can finish my sentence, barks, tails, and paws abound.

Two overzealous pups are greeting the crap out of me, while my furious feline looks down from his perch high atop the stacks.

One pup is tan and compact. He sports a winter sweater festooned with pom-poms. The other is a massive husky with piercing blue eyes, thick blue-black fur, and a white belly.

"Bartles and Jaymes, sit." Twiggy's stern command receives an instant response as she and her biker boots stomp into the hallway.

Two puppers plant their bottoms on the carpet. The smaller one whimpers and fights the urge to launch a second assault of tail wags and tongue licks.

Twiggy towers over the eager dogs. "Now we'll have a proper greeting." She steps beside the smaller dog and makes an "okay" symbol with her left hand. "Say hello, Jaymes." She swings the symbol toward me. Jaymes instantly rises on his back legs and waves his right paw manically.

I reach down and shake his small warm paw. "Good to see you."

By this time Bartles is whining, and his larger rear end is twitching with anticipation.

Jaymes drops onto all fours, and Twiggy gives Bartles the signal. "Say hello to Mitzy."

The black Husky rises on his hind legs, and, when he wiggles his right paw, it nearly reaches my shoulder. I shake it hastily. "Pleased to see you again, Bartles."

He drops, and the two dogs chase each other around the bookstore as Twiggy and I catch up.

"Did everything go okay at the vet the other day?"

She points to the smaller of the two dogs. "Jaymes has gotta go on a diet, and Doc also recommended he stop eating yarn. I didn't even know I had yarn. Not really my thing. But I musta bought some to tie up packages years ago, and this little stinker dug it out. Anyway, he ate enough of it to back him up and give me a little fright. I have to keep an eye on him for a few days to make sure he's healing up okay, but I think we're all good now."

The dogs circle around her when Twiggy snaps her fingers, and she kneels to rub Jaymes' back vigorously as she scolds him in her best "poor baby" voice. "So you're not gonna eat any more yarn, right? And nobody's gonna give me any more heart attacks, right? Who's a good boy? Who's a good boy?"

Both dogs respond to the question with licks and nuzzles.

Pyewacket continues to glare, and a low growl is mounting.

"Don't worry, Pye. We all know you're the *best* boy. That lead with the psychiatrist is paying off in spades, buddy. Extra Fruity Puffs for you tomorrow."

After giving Twiggy a quick briefing, I locate Grams, and we update the murder wall.

My static day, stuck in the cruiser, took more out of me than I thought. I can't get myself into bed soon enough.

However, having left the blackout shades up, the sun prods me out of bed moments before a text arrives from Erick.

"Paulsen is bringing in Dylan Bernard, and Johnson is already on his way back to the station with Dr. Mareno."

"Copy that."

Time for me to slip into something more sleuth-y.

CHAPTER 19

ERICK MEETS ME in the hallway outside the observation room. "I'm going to question Dr. Mareno first. As usual, Dylan Bernard has asked for his lawyer."

"Copy that. Did he say anything before he lawyered up?"

He shakes his head in frustration. "Nope. This guy is a little *too* good. The first time I bought what he was selling, but now I'm not so sure."

"What's that stench?"

Erick juts his thumb toward the interrogation room holding Dylan Bernard. "If you ask me, it smells like a rat."

A few pieces of the puzzle struggle to slide into place. "It reeks. Do you think that was the smell

Raina was describing? Seems like too much of a coincidence that her ex-husband and this Dylan Bernard person would wear the same horrible cologne."

He winks over his shoulder as he grabs the handle of the door leading into Interrogation Room Two. "Exactly."

When I hustle into the observation room, a spine-tingling thought floats to the forefront. Hallucna Jenn never said "ex-*husband.*" I use my psychic recall to replay the conversation. She only said "ex." But in what world is a lowly store clerk dating the owner of a men's wrestling league? This case gets stranger at every turn. When I flip the toggle on, I overhear Erick confirming basic details with Dr. Mareno. But it's the cruel snarl on Dylan Bernard's face in the opposite room that has all of my attention.

He's a man used to getting his way. If this slimy Dylan Bernard is the actual ex Hallucna Jenn was talking about . . . What would a guy like that be doing seeing a therapist? He doesn't exactly strike me as the self-reflective type.

Sheriff Harper seems to have plucked the words from my brain. Time to direct my attention to the interview underway.

As the question regarding Mr. Bernard's client status hangs in the air, Dr. Mareno's face contorts in confusion. "Client? Dylan Bernard is not my client."

Erick lets that rattlesnake lie under a rock for a moment. "Did Tanya Tucker have a discussion with you about her suspicion that you were treating the ex-husband of one of your current female patients?"

Dr. Mareno presses a hand to her chest, and her salt-and-pepper curls bob up and down as she exhales and nods. "Oh, that. You had me worried to death. Tanya and I spoke in detail about that particular patient's concerns. I was able to settle Tanya's worries, and I can ease yours as well. I have sixty current patients on the books. And, at this time, not one of them is male. I am not sure which patient made the accusation, but as you know, many of these women are quite troubled. They have suffered severe trauma, and sometimes they misinterpret the data the world provides. I would never take on the ex-husband of a woman under my care. Not simply because it is unethical, Sheriff. As a survivor myself, I would never risk breaking the bond of trust with one of my patients."

From where I'm sitting, every word that comes out of her mouth sounds like the gospel truth. I feel absolutely no indication that she's holding anything back or bending the truth to her purposes. So why in the world —

"Can you tell me what Dylan Bernard was doing in your office?"

Dr. Mareno smiles and glances down at her hands. "Of course. Dylan and I have been seeing each other for almost six months. I know he gets a bad reputation for what he does with the men's wrestling league, but in private, he happens to be a very sweet man. Thoughtful, complimentary, and very respectful of my time."

The frustration gripping Erick's tense shoulders is palpable. He suspends the interview, but asks Dr. Mareno to give him a few minutes after which he'll return to finalize everything.

She nods pleasantly and seems completely un-perturbed.

In a flash, he dives into the observation room. "What am I missing? There's absolutely no way this woman had anything to do with Tanya's murder." Erick throws his arms in the air. "Everyone can't be innocent."

"Do you think you'll be able to get anything out of this Dylan guy?"

"I doubt it. His lawyer will be here any minute, and then we're out of options." He exhales with the force of building anger.

Getting to my feet, I sidle up next to him and lean in, letting my whispers race across his skin.

"You know how clumsy I can be. Always tripping over things, walking into the wrong room —"

Erick's eyes brighten, and he bites his bottom lip. "When I head back in to finish my interview with Dr. Mareno . . . If Deputy Paulsen catches you, I had nothing to do with it."

"Absolutely. These lips are sealed, Sheriff."

He exits. I count to three, and step into the hallway.

It hardly takes any acting on my part to trip over my own feet and stumble into Interrogation Room One.

"Oh my gosh! Are you Deputy Johnson?"

The man glances up from his phone in irritation, but once he catches sight of my curves, an eager smile curls the corner of his thin lips. "I wish I was. To what do I owe this pleasure?"

Continuing with my ditzy blonde routine, I grab a seat on the table and lean toward him invitingly. "You look like you'd make a great deputy. I bet if you were in charge, you'd have me in handcuffs in no time."

He chuckles greedily, and as he leans toward me, his foul cologne wafts up my nostrils. *Uffda!* It takes every ounce of my pathetic acting ability to keep from tossing my cookies on the floor.

Dylan notices the cooling of my advance, and

he pushes for an advantage. "You look too good for a place like this. What are you in for?"

"So, you're not going to believe this! They think I had something to do with this murder at the dry cleaner's!"

His entire energy shifts. One minute he's a bubbling cauldron about to spill over, and the next, an ice-cold slab of granite.

I gesture to my person and continue. "I mean, look at me. Do I look like a murderer?"

He's struggling to contain a waterfall of emotions behind his faceplate. Dylan knows something. He's tied to it somehow. There's a flash of imagery, but the harder I reach, the tighter he closes up. Before I can make a second attempt, the door opens and the short and stout Deputy Paulsen waddles in. "What are you doing in here?"

Before she can blow my cover, I stumble toward her, put a hand on her shoulder, and exclaim, "I have no idea. Total wrong turn."

I bumble past her and the waiting lawyer, and stand in the hallway like a confused rabbit.

As soon as the lawyer enters the interrogation room, I dart back into the observation room. I didn't get much of anything, but if Erick asks the right questions, he might be able to dislodge a kernel of truth.

Wait, was that image a flash of an owl?

Sheriff Harper finishes with Dr. Mareno and offers to escort her to the front desk.

Attempting to wait patiently, I let my mind wander over the puzzling case.

I'm sure that snippet from Dylan's brain was an owl. That places him at the murder scene. I have to tell the sheriff.

Jumping to my feet, I reach for the door handle, but two things stop me in my tracks. Erick enters the room where Dylan Bernard is waiting, and Deputy Johnson escorts Hallucna Jenn into the other room.

He leaves her alone, and I can sense her fear and desperation mounting. I know she's going to do something foolish. I'd love to know what's on the paper in Erick's hand, but I have to choose the greater emergency.

I hope I won't regret this.

Stepping into the hallway, I turn right and let myself into the interrogation room, much to the shock and awe of Hallucna Jenn.

Dropping all pretense of Cherry Darling and her accent, I spill my guts to the terrified woman. "Look, Raina, I haven't been completely honest with you."

Her mouth hangs open for a moment, and she points toward me. "What happened to your accent?"

"That's just a character. I'm not from Texas. I live here, in Pin Cherry Harbor. Name's Mitzy Moon. Tanya was a dear friend of the family, and I'm determined to find the person responsible for her murder."

Raina's emotional walls rise in a flash. "I'm sick and tired of liars."

"I know you are. And I'm sorry I couldn't be honest with you. I had no idea who was responsible until now. If you can just answer a couple of questions —"

"Why should I help you?"

"You're not helping me. You're helping Tanya, Pilar, and their two innocent children."

That last part does the trick. Loraina tears up and silently nods.

"When you said 'ex,' you weren't talking about your ex-husband, were you?"

She shakes her head.

"Were you dating Dylan Bernard?"

Her eyes widen, and a hand covers her mouth, but eventually, she nods.

"Don't take this the wrong way, but why was he dating you, Raina?"

She seems to take no additional offense. "When I first got to town, I won a bunch of money at the casino. I was living kind of lavishly when I ran into him. He thought I had money. He just used me."

"Why does he care whether or not you have money? He's loaded, isn't he?"

"No way. I saw behind the curtain. He's in deep debt. Those legal actions he keeps taking against the women's wrestling league, and all the money he blows on event promotions . . . He was leveraged like crazy."

"Why did you break up with him?"

"He broke up with me. I should've ditched him after the first time he hit me." Silent tears roll down her cheeks, and I reach across the table to grip her hand comfortingly.

Raina pulls away and eyes me suspiciously. "Why should I trust you? You could be working for him."

"I'm absolutely not working for him! But I am engaged to the sheriff. We saw Dylan Bernard going into Dr. Mareno's office. You were right. He was in that office, but not as a patient. She isn't treating him. They're an item."

My revelation does the trick. She leans forward and gasps. "He's just using her! You have to warn Dr. Mareno. She's — I think she's probably a good person. Dylan just wants to get his hands on her money."

"Did he ever say anything about Tanya when you were dating?"

"All the time. That's why I was so eager to stick

it to him and join the women's wrestling league after we broke up. I wanted to teach him a lesson."

The sound of shallow breathing fills the small space, and I ask my final question. "How violent is he, Raina?"

A sudden realization dawns and her eyes widen in horror. "Do you think —?"

Swallowing loudly, I nod my head. "Unfortunately, that's exactly what I think."

CHAPTER 20

Launching myself into the hallway with a single purpose, I run directly into Deputy Johnson.

"Sorry, I need the sheriff."

The deputy grins sarcastically.

Before he can make a quip about my love life, I head him off at the pass. "It's about the case. It's urgent."

Deputy Johnson throws a thumb over his shoulder. "I just saw him in his office."

Rushing past him, I offer a hasty thanks as I dart into the office.

"It's Dylan!"

Erick crosses his arms and nods. "I agree. What's your reasoning?"

He agrees? Well, that was easy. "He was dating Raina for her money — when she had money — and now he's dating Dr. Mareno to get his slimy hands on her money. He must've realized that Tanya and Raina could sabotage his whole plan if the doctor learned the truth about his relationship with Raina and how he used her money and abused her physically."

The sheriff gets to his feet and reaches out his right hand.

I grip his outstretched hand in confusion and chuckle as he shakes my hand. "That's some good deductive reasoning, Moon. But I have actual evidence. Or I will have in a few minutes. I got a judge to sign the order for Dylan Bernard's DNA and to force him to surrender his gloves."

"His gloves?"

"Yeah. Our genius ME found a tiny shred of mahogany kidskin leather stuck in the macramé fibers of that owl. If we can match that bit to Dylan's custom driving gloves, we've got him."

A huge smile lifts my spirits. "Well, what are you waiting for? Get in there and grab his gloves and stuff."

"Already done. His lawyer was furious, but they had to comply. Paulsen took the gloves and the sample to the lab herself." He glances at his watch and rubs his hands in expectation. "Geez. How long does it take to look at a pair of gloves? Maybe I should call the ME."

"Wow. For a guy who thinks patience is such a virtue, you're coming off a little edgy, Harper."

He exhales, wipes a hand across his forehead, and drops into his chair. "You're right. I'm sure Paulsen is cracking the whip harder than I ever have."

"All right. Why don't I grab you a coffee and see if there are any doughnuts left? Sound good?"

He nods distractedly.

When I return with the cup of liquid tar that passes for coffee in the station and no doughnut, he's on the phone and his eyes shine as brightly as a child's on Christmas morning.

He hangs up the phone and slams his fist on the desk. "We got him."

I'm not sure why I burst into tears, but I can't wait to tell Pilar that her family will get the closure they were waiting for.

Erick hustles around the desk and circles his arms around me. "This was a little too close to home, huh? Are you gonna be okay?"

"Yeah. Is it alright if I go see Pilar?"

"Absolutely. Give her my condolences, will ya?"

"Of course."

Running back toward the Bell, Book & Candle, I dash down my alley and hop into the Jeep. I let my psychic recall lead the way to Pilar's house.

The powers that be are smiling down on me,

and I make it to her house before the children arrive home from school.

She looks about the same as when I left her. Perhaps the bags under her eyes are a little deeper and a darker hue of purple.

"Mitzy. I'm so glad it's you, and not —"

"Pilar, we got him. We've got the man who did this in custody. We have evidence, motive, everything. I'm sure it won't be an open-and-shut case, but the sheriff is very confident. Dylan Bernard is gonna pay for what he did to Tanya."

Pilar melts into a puddle of tears, and I scoop my arms around her to offer some comfort.

Guiding her toward the living room, I place her on the couch with a box of tissues and head into the kitchen to make some tea. By the time I return with the steaming mug of chamomile, her sobbing has reduced to soft sniffles.

"Here, drink this."

She accepts the cuppa and takes a hesitant sip. "Thank you. Not just for the tea. Thank you for everything you've done for me, for Tanya, and for our family."

Taking a seat beside her, I rub her shoulder and nod. "Are you ready to tell the children?"

"Yeah. They're definitely getting suspicious. It's never easy raising intelligent children. They grew up learning to question things, rely on their intuition, and speak up when they have concerns. It's definitely time to tell them the truth. But I can't tell you what a difference it will make to let them know there's at least some justice in the world."

"I'm so glad I could help."

"We're having a memorial for Tanya this weekend. I know you really didn't know her, but you've been so instrumental in solving this case, and your grandmother —"

"My grandmother thought the world of Tanya. I'm happy to say something at the service."

Pilar blows her nose and takes a ragged breath. "Thank you."

ON THE DRIVE BACK TO THE BOOKSTORE, a heaviness descends on my heart. There are too many parallels. A young girl like Lilith losing her mother at such an impressionable age . . . I can't help but flashback to that moment when the police officer knocked on our door in Arizona and gave my babysitter the horrible news.

Although, there are also several things that make Lilith's situation quite different from my childhood. She has a feisty brother to keep her company and a living parent to guide and love her through this tragic situation.

In fact, if Lilith is half as brave and smart as she

seems, she'll find an amazing way to honor Tanya's memory and continue to give back to the community.

All hopes of that positive spin lifting my spirits burst like an over-inflated balloon. The only thing that might possibly do the trick is an actual spirit.

"I need Grams."

My footsteps are heavy in the fresh snow, and I barely notice the piles of rubble and lumber littering the alleyway. I've been so distracted. I haven't even had time to check on the progress of the remodel. Having a gorgeous three-story home for Erick and me to call our own seemed like the most important thing . . . Until I saw Tanya lying on the floor of the dry cleaner's.

Now I can't seem to get rid of this pain in my heart.

When I open the heavy metal doorway, I blast directly into the glowing ghost of Myrtle Isadora. Instead of feeling frustrated and micromanaged, I fling my arms around her semi-corporeal form and sob.

"Mitzy, sweetie. What happened? Are you injured? Did something happen with Erick?"

She continues to fire a barrage of questions as I attempt to get my weeping and breathing under control.

Through my shaky breaths, I manage part of an

explanation. "You're the best thing that ever happened to me, Grams. I'll never be able to truly thank you for all the ways you've changed my life."

Never let it be said that Ghost-ma lacks intuition. "Oh, sweetie. I know it must've been awfully hard for you to work through this case, knowing there were children involved. But none of us are promised tomorrow. What you did for that family will make all the difference. So you take a deep breath and remember that you are Mizithra Achelois Moon. Heiress, business owner, and philanthropist."

As the words sink into my tender heart, a flash of inspiration finally blows the grey clouds away.

"That's it! You're a genius! I'm going to ask Silas to set up a women's sports fund. The Duncan-Moon Foundation can finance the women's wrestling league and maybe set up a couple of athletic scholarships for girls at the high school. One can be for female hockey players!" Spinning around and taking a cleansing breath, I exhale and smile through my tears. "See, Grams. You absolutely bring out the best in me."

Pyewacket crashes into the back of my leg and drops something at my feet.

Glancing down at the plushy owl, now missing one of his plastic eyes, a chuckle clears the last bit of my sadness away.

Crouching, I pick up the owl in one hand and scratch the majestic caracal's head with the other. "Once again, Robin Pyewacket Goodfellow, I never would've solved the case without your clues. You're an invaluable member of the Scooby Gang and don't you ever forget it."

"Reow." Can confirm.

CHAPTER 21

Once Dylan Bernard was arrested and confronted with the evidence, he threw Cobb Astley at the sheriff's feet like a sacrificial lamb. My brilliant fiancé parleyed that into convincing Astley to turn state's evidence on Bernard, and got himself an inside guy to testify to Dylan's hatred of Tanya Tucker. Means. Motive. Opportunity.

Erick will be tied up with paperwork until quite late. No time like the present to check on the progress of the remodel.

As I push through the "Employees Only" door into what used to be our printing museum, the name Silas Willoughby pops unbidden into my head.

Placing the call on speaker, I ring my mentor.

"Good afternoon, Mr. Willoughby. I thought

you might like to hear how I got on with the videotapes."

"It is always a pleasure to hear from you, Mitzy. I should consider it an honor to be updated on your growing powers. Please, elucidate me."

His ridiculous vocabulary brings a chuckle, and I fill him in on the pertinent details of my psychic videotape review and our subsequent arrest of Tanya's murderer.

"Fantastic. I couldn't be more pleased with your progress. Was there anything else?"

"And you keep telling me you're not psychic, Silas. There is something else. I'd like to set up a fund for the women's wrestling league, in Tanya's name. I think it's what she would've wanted. And I'd like to set up a couple of girls' athletic scholarships at the high school. One needs to be specifically for hockey."

He harrumphs, and I hear a pen scratching across paper on his end of the line. "Will that be all, Mizithra?"

"That's it for now. Although you may want to bring Pyewacket a special treat on your next visit. I'm not sure whether it was just this case, or possibly his powers are growing as well, but he certainly put together some valuable clues on this one."

"Indeed. Pyewacket remains a mystery for the ages."

"Thanks for your help, Silas. I better let you go. I need to get my head around this remodel to make sure things are on track."

"Of course. And how are things progressing on plans for the wedding of the century?"

His obvious dig at Ghost-ma's tendency to go overboard brings a full-on belly laugh. I'm forced to place my hand on my knee to support myself as I struggle to catch my breath.

"Wow! You're not just whistling Dixie. If it wouldn't break Isadora's heart, I'd be sorely tempted to elope. Hopefully, there will be a moment or two of sanity during the day. I'd like to think it's about me and Erick, but at this point, it feels very much like it's all about Grams."

Silas exhales loudly into the phone. "If you haven't yet been nominated for sainthood, it is not a struggle to imagine that if you survive your wedding day, your name will move very close to the top of the list. The pope is a personal friend, if you'd like me to put in a good word." He barely finishes his sentence before deep guffaws suspend the teasing.

I can easily imagine his jiggling jowls and reddened cheeks. "On that note, I'll let you go, Mr. Willoughby."

He offers a formal goodbye, and the call ends.

As I make my way through the construction

site, a gentle vision swirls up my spine and fills my mind.

I can see past all the debris, dust, and tarps. Lights shine brightly in my open-plan kitchen/living room, and an inviting fire crackles in the fireplace.

From my vantage point, stretched out on a cozy sofa in front of a warming blaze, I can smell heavenly aromas in the kitchen.

Lifting my head to peer over the sofa in my vision, I see Erick hard at work. He wears an apron covered with stains, and he whistles while he prepares our dinner.

"Whatcha makin', Sheriff?"

His deep blue eyes sing with love as he gazes across the room. "As promised, I'm making my world-famous lasagna for my beautiful bride."

His beautiful bride? That's me!

I've never had a vision of things so far in the future. Maybe it's one of my silly daydreams. I'm sure I'm just filling in what I want to see, not actually visualizing the future.

A ringing phone interrupts the images, but it's not mine. It's in the vision.

Erick picks up his phone from the granite countertop and speaks in hushed tones into the receiver. He ends the call and gazes across the room with concern and a hint of excitement.

"What's up, Ricky?"

"You better get suited up, Moon. We've got a case."

How weird. Normally, I have to worm my way into his cases. Not to mention, he was very clear about sleuthing not being a proper profession for a sheriff's wife.

Well, no *Inception* top needed. This is clearly a fantasy of my own making, not an actual premonition.

Oh well, I'll take visions of Sheriff Too-Hot-To-Handle any way I can get them.

End of Prequel (Book 0.5)

But, the mysteries continue...
Curl up with the next book in the Harper and
Moon Investigations series!

I can't wait for their next case! I hope you're ready to join Mitzy and Erick on their new adventures in **Harper and Moon Investigations**. As always, I'll keep writing them if you keep reading . . .

The best part of "living" in Pin Cherry Harbor continues to be feedback from my early readers. Thank you to my alpha readers/cheerleaders, Angel and Michael. HUGE thanks to my fantastic beta readers who continue to give me extremely useful and honest feedback: Veronica McIntyre and Nadine Peterse-Vrijhof. And big "small town" hugs to the world's best ARC Team – Trixie's Mystery ARC Detectives!

My wonderful editor Philip Newey definitely helped me sort out the timeline. Many thanks to him! I enjoy getting notes and polishing each case.

I'd also like to give piles of gratitude to Roxx at Proof Perfect for the stellar proofing! Any remaining errors are my own.

And finally, my heart is full of gratitude for the real-life Lilith, who gave me permission to use her name and a sliver of her life as inspiration for a character. The page could not hold all the details of this wunderkind! Thank you, Lil.

FUN FACT: My grandmother lasted three minutes in the ring with Gorilla Monsoon — before he joined the WWF. LOL! Apparently, that was a whole "thing" at county fairs back in the day.

My favorite line from this case: "Time for me to slip into something more sleuth-y." ~Mitzy

I'm currently writing book two in the **Harper and Moon Investigations** series, *Rodeo Clowns and Shakedowns*. All your *Mitzy Moon Mysteries* series favorites will continue on—but there will be a few "shake ups" in town.

I hope you'll continue to hang out with us.

Trixie Silvertale (February 2023)

Harper and Moon Investigations No. 1

A pattern of murder. A threadbare case. Can our psychic sleuth pick out the guilty before time spools out?

Mitzy Moon is finally tying the knot. And she's loving the whole town's excitement for their upcoming big day. But when their tailor is found buttons up behind a jazz lounge, the almost-newlyweds will have to hem in a murderer before their dreams rip apart at the seams.

Knowing they'll get no help from the new sheriff in town, the couple embarks on a tightly woven undercover assignment. But Mitzy fails to heed ominous warnings from her mentor, Ghost-ma, and her entitled feline. When another body drops, she could be the next target erased by the mounting powers in the darkness...

Can Mitzy and Erick unravel the twisted clues, or will their wedding be eclipsed by a funeral?

Bells and Bombshells is the first book in a hilarious new paranormal cozy mystery series, Harper and Moon Investigations. If you like snarky heroines, supernatural intrigue, and a dash of romance, then you'll love Trixie Silvertale's wedded whodunit.

Buy *Bells and Bombshells* to stitch up a killer today!

Grab yours!
https://readerlinks.com/l/5211927

Scan this QR Code with the camera on your phone. You'll be taken right to the next Harper and Moon Investigations case.

Once you're in the Club, you'll also be the first to receive updates from Pin Cherry Harbor and access to giveaways, new release announcements, short stories, behind-the-scenes secrets, and much more!

Scan this QR Code with the camera on your phone. You'll be taken right to the page to join the Club!

Thank you kindly, and I'll see you in Pin Cherry Harbor!

Mitzy Moon Mysteries

Fries and Alibis: Paranormal Cozy Mystery

Tattoos and Clues: Paranormal Cozy Mystery

Wings and Broken Things: Paranormal Cozy Mystery

Sparks and Landmarks: Paranormal Cozy Mystery

Charms and Firearms: Paranormal Cozy Mystery

Bars and Boxcars: Paranormal Cozy Mystery

Swords and Fallen Lords: Paranormal Cozy Mystery

Wakes and High Stakes: Paranormal Cozy Mystery

Tracks and Flashbacks: Paranormal Cozy Mystery

Lies and Pumpkin Pies: Paranormal Cozy Mystery

Hopes and Slippery Slopes: Paranormal Cozy Mystery

Hearts and Dark Arts: Paranormal Cozy Mystery

Dames and Deadly Games: Paranormal Cozy Mystery

Castaways and Longer Days: Paranormal Cozy Mystery

Schemes and Bad Dreams: Paranormal Cozy Mystery

Carols and Yule Perils: Paranormal Cozy Mystery

Dangers and Empty Mangers: Paranormal Cozy Mystery

Heists and Poltergeists: Paranormal Cozy Mystery

Blades and Bridesmaids: Paranormal Cozy Mystery

Scones and Tombstones: Paranormal Cozy Mystery

Vandals and Yule Scandals: Paranormal Cozy Mystery

Harper and Moon Investigations

Ropes and Last Hopes: Paranormal Cozy Mystery

Bells and Bombshells: Paranormal Cozy Mystery

Rodeo Clowns and Shakedowns: Paranormal Cozy Mystery

Stiffs and Petroglyphs: Paranormal Cozy Mystery

Fatal Wines and Valentines: Paranormal Cozy Mystery

April Curses and May Hearses: Paranormal Cozy Mystery

Wheels and Dirty Deals: Paranormal Cozy Mystery

Scripts and Empty Crypts: Paranormal Cozy Mystery

Christmas Catastrophe Mysteries

Peppermint Cookie Murder: Paranormal Cozy Mystery

Apple Dumpling Murder: Paranormal Cozy Mystery

Linzer Cookie Murder: Paranormal Cozy Mystery

Chocolate Crinkle Cookie Murder: Paranormal Cozy Mystery

...more to come!

Explore the world of Coriander the Conjurer. A fortune-telling fairy with a heart of gold!

Book 1:

All Swell That Ends Spell – A dubious festival. A fatal swim. Can this fortune-telling fairy herald the true killer?

Book 2:

Fairy Wives of Windsor – A jolly Faire. A shocking murder. Can this furtive fairy outsmart the killer?

Book 3:

Double Double Royal Trouble – When a treat-peddling witch is found dead, will this cursed faire crumble?

Join Sydney Coleman and her unruly ghosts, as they solve mysteries in a truly haunted mansion!

Book 1: ***Moonlight and Mischief*** – She's desperate for a fresh start, but is a mansion on sale too good to be true?

Book 2: ***Moonlight and Magic*** – A haunted Halloween tour seem like the perfect plan, until there's murder...

Book 3: ***Moonlight and Mayhem*** – An unwelcome visitor. A surprising past. Will her fire sale end in smoke?

USA TODAY Bestselling author Trixie Silvertale grew up reading an endless supply of Lilian Jackson Braun, Hardy Boys, and Nancy Drew novels. She loves the amateur sleuths in cozy mysteries and obsesses about all things paranormal. Those two passions unite in her Harper and Moon Investigations, and she's thrilled to write them and share them with you.

When she's not consumed by writing, she bakes to fuel her creative engine and pulls weeds in her herb garden to clear her head (*and sometimes she pulls out her hair, but mostly weeds*).

Greetings are welcome:
trixie@trixiesilvertale.com

bookbub.com/authors/trixie-silvertale

facebook.com/TrixieSilvertale

instagram.com/trixiesilvertale

Made in the USA
Monee, IL
07 July 2026